U0092794

基礎文法寶典 ④
Essential English Usage & Grammar

編著／J. B. Alter
審訂／劉美皇　呂香瑩

Grammar Guru

三民書局

國家圖書館出版品預行編目資料

Essential English Usage & Grammar 基礎文法寶典
／J. B. Alter編著;劉美皇,呂香瑩審訂.－－初版
一刷.－－臺北市：三民，2008
　　冊；　公分

　　ISBN 978-957-14-5104-6　（平裝）
　　1. 英語 2. 語法

805.16　　　　　　　　　　　　　　97018552

© **Essential English Usage & Grammar**
基礎文法寶典 4

編 著 者	J. B. Alter
審　　訂	劉美皇　呂香瑩
企劃編輯	王伊平
責任編輯	彭彥哲
美術設計	郭雅萍

發 行 人	劉振強
著作財產權人	三民書局股份有限公司
發 行 所	三民書局股份有限公司
	地址　臺北市復興北路386號
	電話　(02)25006600
	郵撥帳號　0009998-5
門 市 部	（復北店）臺北市復興北路386號
	（重南店）臺北市重慶南路一段61號

出版日期	初版一刷　2008年11月
編　　號	S 807530

行政院新聞局登記證局版臺業字第○二○○號

ISBN　978-957-14-5104-6　（平裝）

http://www.sanmin.com.tw　三民網路書店
※本書如有缺頁、破損或裝訂錯誤，請寄回本公司更換。

序

如果說，單字是英文的血肉，文法就是英文的骨架。想要打好英文基礎，兩者實應相輔相成，缺一不可。

只是，單字可以死背，文法卻不然。

學習文法，如果沒有良師諄諄善誘，沒有好書細細剖析，只落得個見樹不見林，徒然勞心費力，實在可惜。

Guru 原義指的是精通於某領域的「達人」，因此，這一套「文法 Guru」系列叢書，本著 Guru「導師」的精神，要告訴您：親愛的，我把英文文法變簡單了！

「文法 Guru」系列，適用對象廣泛，從初習英文的超級新鮮人、被文法糾纏得寢食難安的中學生，到鎮日把玩英文的專業行家，都能在這一套系列叢書中找到最適合自己的夥伴。

深願「文法 Guru」系列，能成為您最好的學習夥伴，伴您一同輕鬆悠遊英文學習的美妙世界。

有了「文法 Guru」，文法輕鬆上路！

前言

　　「**基礎文法寶典**」一套五冊，是專為中學生與一般社會大眾所設計，作為基礎課程教材或是課外自學之用。

　　英語教師往往對結構、句型、語法等為主的教學模式再熟悉不過。然而，現在學界普遍意識到**文法在語言學習的過程中亦佔有一席之地**，少了文法這一環，英語教學便顯得空洞。有鑑於此，市場上漸漸興起一股「**功能性文法**」的風潮。功能性文法旨在列舉用法並協助讀者熟悉文法專有名詞，而後者便是用以解釋及界定一語言各種功能的利器。

　　本套書各冊內容編排詳盡，涵蓋所有用法及文法要點；除此之外，本套書最強調的便是從不斷的練習中學好英文。每章所附的練習題皆經特別設計，提供讀者豐富多元的演練題型，舉凡**完成** (completion)、**修正** (modification)、**轉換** (conversion)、**合併** (integration)、**重述** (restatement)、**改寫** (alteration)、**變形** (transformation) 及**代換** (transposition)，應有盡有。

　　熟讀此書，將可幫助您完全理解各種文法及正確的表達方式，讓您在課業學習或日常生活上的英文程度突飛猛進。

給讀者的話

本書一套共五本，共分為二十一章，從最基礎的各式詞類介紹，一直到動詞的進階應用、基本書寫概念等，涵蓋所有的基本文法要義，為您建立一個完整的自修體系，並以豐富多樣的練習題為最大特色。

本書的主要細部單元包括：

USAGE PRACTICE →每個文法條目說明之下，皆有大量的例句或用法實例，讓您充分了解該文法規則之實際應用方式。

注意→很多文法規則皆有特殊的應用，或者是因應不同情境而產生相關變化，這些我們都以較小字的提示，列在本單元中。

但是我們會用→文法規則的例外情況也不少，我們在這單元直接以舉例的方式，說明這些不依循規則的情況。

小練習→每節介紹後，會有針對該節內容所設計的一段習題，可讓您即時驗證前面所學的內容。

應用練習→每章的內容結束後，我們都提供了非常充分的應用練習，而且題型豐富，各有其學習功能。建議您不要急於在短時間內將練習做完，而是漸進式地逐步完成，這樣可達成更好的學習效果。

本書文法內容完善，習題亦兼具廣度與深度，是您自修學習之最佳選擇，也可作為文法疑難的查閱參考，值得您細細研讀，慢慢體會。

基礎文法寶典 ❹
Essential English Usage & Grammar

目次

基礎文法寶典 ❹
Essential English Usage & Grammar

Chapter 13 助動詞

13-0 基本概念

助動詞包括：be、do、have、shall、will、can、may、must、need、dare、ought to、used to 等，其用法與一般動詞不同，變化也較無規則。有些助動詞同時也可以當普通動詞使用，所以要小心分辨。

13-1 助動詞的用法

(a) 助動詞用來表示時態。

USAGE PRACTICE
▶ She **is** sleeping now. 她現在正在睡覺。（現在進行式）
▶ She **has** gone home. 她已經回家了。（現在完成式）
▶ I **will** watch them. 我會看著他們。（未來簡單式）

(b) 助動詞放在句首形成疑問句。

USAGE PRACTICE
▶ **Can** he speak English? 他會說英文嗎？
▶ **Does** it work? 這有效嗎？
▶ **Did** you ask her? 你問她了嗎？

(c) 助動詞與 not 結合形成否定句。

USAGE PRACTICE
▶ They **will** not come. 他們不會來。
▶ He **won't** obey you. 他不會服從你。
▶ She **may** not enter. 她可能不會進來。
▶ I **mustn't** interrupt them now. 我現在不能打斷他們。

(d) 助動詞用來加強語氣。

USAGE PRACTICE

▶ I **do** like you. 我真的喜歡你。

▶ **Do** sit down. 坐下。

13-2 be 動詞

原形	be	
	現在式	過去式
第一人稱單數	am	was
第三人稱單數	is	was
第二人稱單數、各人稱的複數	are	were
現在分詞	being	
過去分詞	been	

(a) 含 be 動詞的肯定句轉成否定句和疑問句。

USAGE PRACTICE

肯定句	否定句	疑問句
▶ I am reading.	→ I am not reading.	→ Am I reading?
我正在閱讀。	我不是正在閱讀。	我正在閱讀嗎？
▶ She is running.	→ She isn't running.	→ Is she running?
她正在跑步。	她不是正在跑步。	她正在跑步嗎？
▶ They are here.	→ They aren't here.	→ Are they here?
他們在這裡。	他們不在這裡。	他們在這裡嗎？
▶ He was asleep.	→ He wasn't asleep.	→ Was he asleep?
他當時睡著了。	他當時沒睡著。	他當時有睡著嗎？
▶ You were there.	→ You weren't there.	→ Were you there?
你當時在那裡。	你當時不在那裡。	你當時在那裡嗎？

 注意 be 動詞常和 not 縮寫成一個字，例如 is not 寫成 isn't、was not 寫成 wasn't、are not 寫成 aren't、were not 寫成 weren't。請特別注意 am not 沒有正式的縮寫用法。

(b) be 動詞可以與現在分詞形成所有時態的進行式。

▶ I **am** leaving. 我正要離開。（現在進行式）

▶ I **am** telling you the truth. 我正在告訴你真相。（現在進行式）

▶ We **are** going to the museum. 我們正要去博物館。（現在進行式）

▶ I **was** reading when he entered. 當他進來時，我正在看書。（過去進行式）

▶ He **wasn't being** rude to you just now. 他剛才沒有對你很粗魯。（過去進行式）

▶ She will **be** coming home soon. 她很快就會回家。（未來進行式）

(c) be 動詞可以與過去分詞形成被動語態。

▶ She **is** invited to the tea party. 她被邀請去茶會。

▶ These spoons **are** made well. 這些湯匙做得很好。

▶ He **was** beaten by a thug. 他被暴徒打了。

▶ The window **was** broken and the curtains **were** torn. 窗戶被打破，窗簾也被撕破。

▶ They **were** asked to resign. 他們被要求辭職。

(d) 當 be 動詞後面接不定詞時，表示「之前已經安排好要做的事情」或「傳達指令」。

▶ I **am** to accompany my mother to Wakkanai tomorrow. 我明天將要陪我媽媽去稚內。

▶ She **is** to attend the reception this afternoon. 她今天下午將要參加歡迎會。

▶ He **is** to be transferred to the border. 他將要被送到邊界去。

▶ He **is** not to enter that room. 他不可進入那個房間。

▶ She **is** to help you with your work. 她會幫你做你的工作。

▶ We **are** to meet her at the station. 我們將要在車站和她見面。

▶ You **are** not to leave without permission. 沒有允許你不可以離開。

▶ You **are** to be on duty from now on. 從現在開始，你要值班。

▶ They **are** to report for work tomorrow. 明天他們將要報到上班。

 當用在過去式時，表示「原先安排好的事情並未被執行」。

▶ She **was** to meet us here, but she did not turn up. 她本來要在這裡和我們碰面，但她沒出現。

▶ She **was** to help you with your work. 她本來要幫你做你的工作的。（但她沒有）

▶ He **was** to have informed us, but he forgot. 他本來應該已經要通知我們了，但是他忘了。

▶ They **were** to come this weekend, but they couldn't make it.
他們本來這週末要來，但他們沒能來。

▶ They **were** to have gone earlier, but they were delayed. 他們本來要早點離開，但是被耽誤了。

(e) be 動詞的祈使句表示「命令」，其用法與其他一般動詞的祈使句相同，可用 do 來
加強語氣或用 don't 來表示否定。

USAGE PRACTICE

▶ **Be** back early! 早點回來！

▶ **Be** punctual! 要準時！

▶ **Be** quiet! 安靜點！

▶ **Be** ready at eight o'clock. 八點時務必要準備好！

▶ Do **be** quick. 快點。

▶ Don't **be** late. 別遲到。

 小練習

請在空格中填入正確的 be 動詞形式。

1. She _____ to buy the tickets for us today.

2. You _____ not careful about your work. I can see many mistakes in it.

3. He _____ to report the matter to the teacher at once.

4. As she _____ driving home, it started to rain.

5. He _____ wounded in a gun battle last month.

6. His plans _____ approved by the authorities last week.

7. She _____ ready to go with you in an hour.

8. _____ you angry with me for what I did yesterday?

9. I _____ to tell you that the game has been canceled.

10. They _____ going to tell us when you came in.

11. I _____ not writing any letters today.

12. The doctor _____ here an hour ago.

13. We _____ to stay in the house until he comes back.

14. They _____ dressing for the party when they _____ informed of the news yesterday.

15. Those flats _____ built in 1965. Now they _____ up for sale. _____ anybody living in them now?

☞ 更多相關習題請見本章應用練習 Part 1。

13-3 have

原形	have	
	現在式	過去式
第一、二人稱單數、各人稱的複數	have	had
第三人稱單數	has	had
現在分詞	having	
過去分詞	had	

(a) 助動詞 have 可以和過去分詞構成完成式。

USAGE PRACTICE

▶ I **have** taken the keys. 我帶了鑰匙。（現在完成式）

▶ I **have** told her what to do. 我已經告訴她要做什麼。（現在完成式）

▶ He **has** forgotten to bring his glasses. 他忘了帶他的眼鏡。（現在完成式）

▶ She **has** spoken to him about it. 她已經跟他說過那件事了。（現在完成式）

▶ I **have** been told to leave. 我已經被告知要離開。（現在完成式的被動語態）

▶ He **has** been asked to come. 他已經被要求要來。（現在完成式的被動語態）

▶ I **had** heard the story before. 我以前聽過這個故事。（過去完成式）

▶ They **had** already tidied up their rooms. 他們已經把他們的房間收拾好了。（過去完成式）

▶ The train will **have** gone by the time you reach there.

你到那裡時，火車將已經開走了。（未來完成式）

▶ They will **have** finished the report in an hour.

他們在一小時內將已經完成報告。（未來完成式）

 注意 have 當助動詞時常和 not 縮寫成一個字，例如 have not 寫成 haven't、has not 寫成 hasn't、had not 寫成 hadn't。

基礎文法寶典❹
Essential English Usage & Grammar

(b) have 可以單獨當一般動詞使用，表示「（擁）有」或「處於某一個特殊的狀況」。

USAGE PRACTICE

▶ He **has** a new watch. 他有一支新手錶。

▶ He doesn't **have** much money with him. 他沒有帶很多錢。

▶ How many sisters do you **have**? 你有幾個姊妹？

▶ Don't you **have** any relatives at all? 你一個親戚也沒有嗎？

▶ Do you often **have** colds? 你常感冒嗎？

▶ That truck **has** eight wheels. 那部卡車有八個車輪。

▶ Does your cat **have** a long tail? 你的貓有長的尾巴嗎？

▶ A square **has** four sides of equal length. 正方形有等長的四邊。

▶ A circle **has** no corners. 圓沒有角。

▶ They **have** a spare bed in that room. 他們在那個房間裡有一張空床。

注意　have 當一般動詞時，還可以表示以下涵義。

▶ I **had** (= ate) my lunch just now. 我剛剛吃了午餐。

▶ Did you **have** (= receive) a letter from home? 你收到家裡寄來的信了嗎？

▶ She doesn't **have** (= experience/find) much difficulty in learning foreign languages.
她在學習外語上沒有太多困難。

 小練習

請在空格中填入一般動詞或助動詞 have，並注意必要的變化。

1. My sister _____ a headache. She's lying down in bed.

2. There _____ been no one who can beat him at that!

3. We _____ a picnic by the waterfall last weekend.

4. They _____ dinner at half past seven every evening.

5. Peter _____ a bath when his friend came to see him.

6. The museum _____ attracted a lot of tourists since it was built.

7. She _____ never been to such a large city and thus she was frightened.

8. Do you _____ a few coins to lend me? I want to make a telephone call.

9. My uncle, who _____ a large Alsatian, never locks his doors at night.

10. Everyone _____ gone home except me.

11. Neither of them _____ seen my pen anywhere around.

12. It is eight o'clock. Mr. Reyes and his family _____ breakfast.

13. Each of us _____ habits which we are not aware of.

14. Susie's pet rabbit _____ white fur and a pair of red eyes.

15. Mr. Jacobs _____ his house painted for Christmas last year.

16. I don't feel well today. I _____ a slight fever.

17. When do we _____ to finish this essay?

18. Don't disturb them. They _____ a discussion in the room.

19. The foreman hurriedly came over and soon _____ the machine under control again.

20. _____ you had enough of these chocolates? Do _____ some more.

☞ 更多相關習題請見本章應用練習 Part 2～Part 3。

13-4 do

原形	do	
	現在式	過去式
第一、二人稱單數、各人稱的複數	do	did
第三人稱單數	does	did
現在分詞	doing	
過去分詞	done	

(a) 利用助動詞 do 來構成否定句和疑問句。

USAGE PRACTICE		
肯定句	否定句	疑問句
▶ They like to eat chocolates. 他們喜歡吃巧克力。	→ They **do not** like to eat chocolates. 他們不喜歡吃巧克力。	→ **Do** they like to eat chocolates? 他們喜歡吃巧克力嗎？
▶ She says that she is tired. 她說她累了。	→ She **does not** say that she is tired. 她沒有說她累了。	→ **Does** she say that she is tired? 她說她累了嗎？

▶ He finished the work by himself. 他獨自完成這工作。	→ He **did not** finish the work by himself. 他不是獨自完成這工作。	→ **Did** he finish the work by himself? 他獨自完成這工作嗎？
▶ He wishes to go on the excursion. 他想去遠足。	→ He **does not** wish to go on the excursion. 他不想去遠足。	→ **Does** he wish to go on the excursion? 他想去遠足嗎？

▶ **Do** I look pale? 我看起來很蒼白嗎？

▶ She **doesn't** have to worry at all. 她一點也不用擔心。

▶ He **didn't** study hard enough. 他讀書不夠努力。

▶ **Didn't** he work with you? 他沒有和你一起工作嗎？

 do 當助動詞時常和 not 縮寫成一個字，例如 do not 寫成 don't、does not 寫成 doesn't、did not 寫成 didn't。

(b) 助動詞 do 可以用在簡答句中，以避免重覆。

USAGE PRACTICE

▶ "Do you want some food?" "No, I **don't**." 「你想要一些食物嗎？」「不，我不要。」

▶ "Do you want to come with us?" "Yes, I **do**./No, I **don't**."

「你想和我們一起來嗎？」「是的，我想。／不，我不想。」

▶ "Did Leon talk too much?" "Yes, he **did**./No, he **didn't**."

「里昂說太多話了嗎？」「是的，他是。／不，他沒有。」

(c) 助動詞 do 可以用來取代前面的動詞（或動詞片語），以避免重覆。

USAGE PRACTICE

▶ They like blue, and so **does** Peter. 他們喜歡藍色，彼得也喜歡。

▶ She wants to go to the party, and so **do** I. 她想去參加派對，我也想去。

▶ I like gardening; so **does** my sister. 我喜歡園藝，我妹妹也喜歡。

▶ I didn't ask him to come; neither **did** she. 我沒有叫他來，她也沒有。

▶ I didn't go there, and neither **did** she. 我沒去那裡，她也沒去。

▶ We asked him to stop the car, but he **didn't**. 我們要他停車，但是他沒有。

▶ She doesn't know how to drive a car, but I **do**. 她不知道怎麼開車，但我知道。

▶ Those who wish to rehearse for the play may **do** so now.

　凡是希望彩排演出的人現在可以彩排了。

▶ You must finish the work in an hour. If you **do** so, I will give you a day off.

　你必須在一小時之內完成這工作，如果你這麼做，我將給你一天假。

(d) 助動詞 do 可以用在附加問句中，取代前面的動詞（或動詞片語），以避免重覆。

USAGE PRACTICE

▶ She says that she is tired, **doesn't** she?　她說她累了，不是嗎？

▶ She **doesn't** say that she is tired, **does** she?　她沒有說她累了，是嗎？

▶ He finished the work by himself, **didn't** he?　他獨自完成這工作的，不是嗎？

▶ He **didn't** finish the work by himself, **did** he?　他不是獨自完成這工作的，是嗎？

▶ He **doesn't** wish to go on the excursion, **does** he?　他不想去遠足，是嗎？

▶ She teaches History, **doesn't** she?　她教歷史，不是嗎？

▶ He didn't speak to you, **did** he?　他沒和你說話，是嗎？

(e) 在肯定句中，可以用助動詞 do 來加強語氣。

USAGE PRACTICE

▶ **Do** take the book if you want to.　如果你想要這本書，你就拿去吧。

▶ **Do** stay with us. We'd love to have you.　請務必留下來。我們很希望能有你的參與。

▶ **Do** tell me all about it.　務必告訴我關於那件事的詳情。

▶ **Do** say that you will come!　務必說你會來！

▶ You **do** work hard when you are forced to.　當你被迫得努力工作的時候，你真的會很賣力。

▶ We **do** boil our water before drinking it, you know.

　你知道的，我們在喝水前真的有先將它煮沸。

▶ She **does** intend to apply, but she doesn't want anyone to know.

　她真的想要申請，但她不想讓任何人知道。

▶ He **did** say something, but I wasn't paying attention to him.

　他的確說了些話，但是我沒注意。

▶ He **did** ask your permission, but you didn't hear him.　他確實有徵求你的允許，但你沒聽到。

(f) do 也可以當作一般動詞使用。

 助動詞 do 要與原形動詞連用，一般動詞 do 則可以單獨使用。

一般動詞 do

▶ He **does** his work well. 他把工作做得很好。

▶ She **did** nothing all day. 她整天什麼都沒做。

▶ The holiday **did** her good. 那假期對她有益。

助動詞 do

▶ He **does** not want to do his work. 他不想工作。

▶ She **didn't** see us. 她沒看見我們。

▶ She **does** look well. 她看起來的確很不錯。

小練習

請在空格中填入一般動詞或助動詞 do（若需否定請用縮寫形式），並注意必要的變化。

1. She ate sandwiches for lunch; so _____ I.

2. I _____ understand what you are saying.

3. They _____ their work very carefully every day.

4. You like eggs, _____ you?

5. If you wish to make a phone call, you may _____ so here.

6. He comes here every day, _____ he?

7. The cakes _____ look delicious, _____ they?

8. She _____ hang out the clothes to dry, _____ she?

9. "_____ you usually have your lunch at one o'clock?" "Yes, I _____."

10. He _____ contribute much to the housekeeping money last year.

11. "_____ he always smoke a packet of cigarettes a day?" "Yes, he _____."

12. I _____ agree with your suggestion. Not everyone likes to swim, _____ they?

13. They told me that Charles failed the test, but he _____ , _____ he?

14. What _____ Mr. Fraser _____ for a living? He inherited his father's property, _____ he?

☞ 更多相關習題請見本章應用練習 Part 4～Part 11。

13-5 shall & should

(a) 助動詞 shall 可以與原形動詞構成未來式，通常與第一人稱代名詞 I 或 we 連用。

USAGE PRACTICE

▶ I **shall** return this book tomorrow. 明天我將要歸還這本書。

▶ We **shall** meet you at one o'clock. 我們將在一點與你碰面。

▶ I **shall** be there in time for the concert. 我將及時到那裡去那聽音樂會。

▶ We **shall** do what we like in our own house. 在我們自己的家裡，我們會做我們喜歡的事。

▶ We **shall** have finished when you return. 當你回來時，我們將會已經完工。

▶ I **shall not** be seeing her next month. 下個月我不會見到她。

▶ We **shall** be visiting our uncle next week. 我們將在下星期拜訪叔叔。

▶ I **shall** be going straight home after work. 我在下班後將直接回家。

 現代用法除了書面文字或特別強調的狀況下，shall 已經很少用來構成未來式，一般都以 will 或 be going to 取代。

▶ I **will** return this book tomorrow. 明天我將要歸還這本書。

▶ We **are going to** meet you at one o'clock. 我們將在一點與你碰面。

(b) should 則是 shall 的過去式。

USAGE PRACTICE

▶ I told him that I **should** be there by noon. 我告訴他我會在中午前到那裡。

▶ He said that we **should** meet at one o'clock. 他說我們將會在一點鐘碰面。

▶ They told me that I **should** have a short holiday next week.

他們告訴我下週我會有一個短的假期。

 shall 或 should 可和 not 縮寫成一個字，例如 shall not 寫成 shan't、should not 寫成 shouldn't。

(c) 助動詞 shall 和 should 也可以用在條件句和假設語氣。

USAGE PRACTICE

▶ If we have nothing to do, we **shall** go to the movies.

如果我們沒什麼事要做，我們會去看電影。

▶ If you wish, we **shall** stay with you. 如果你希望，我們會留下和你在一起。

▶ If I fall ill, I **shall** not go. 如果我生病了，我就不會去。

▶ I **shall** give him your message if I see him. 如果我遇見他，我會把你的口信傳給他。

▶ We **should** be all right in a boat if there is no storm.

如果沒有暴風雨，我們在船上應該很安全。

▶ They **should** be here on Monday unless they are delayed.

除非是被耽擱了，不然星期一他們應該會在這裡。

▶ I **shouldn't** worry if I were you. 如果我是你，我就不會擔心。（假設語氣）

▶ If there were more volunteers, we **should** finish the job in time.

如果有更多的自願者，我們會及時完成工作。

▶ If we had caught the first bus, we **should** have been there on time.

如果我們搭上了第一班公車，我們應該已經準時到那裡了。（假設語氣）

 助動詞 should 用於 if 子句時，表示「對未來強烈懷疑」，作「萬一」解。當從屬連接詞 if 被省略時，助動詞 should 要移到句首形成倒裝句。

▶ If I **should** be free tomorrow, I will come. 萬一明天我有空，我會來。

→ **Should** I be free tomorrow, I will come.

▶ If I should have the money, I would lend it to you. 萬一我有錢，我會借給你。

→ **Should** I have the money, I would lend it to you.

(d) 助動詞 shall 和 should 也可以用來表達「徵求意見」。

USAGE PRACTICE

▶ **Shall** I sign up for the Social Science course? 我要報名參加社會科學課程嗎？

▶ **Shall** I come this evening? 我今天晚上要來嗎？

▶ Which CD **shall** I play now? 我現在要播放哪張 CD 好呢？

▶ Which of these paintings **shall** I buy? 我該買這些畫中的那一幅呢？

▶ What **shall** I do with this parcel? 我要怎麼處理這個包裹呢？

▶ Where **shall** we have lunch? 我們要在哪吃午餐呢？

▶ Whom **should** I invite to the party? 我該邀請誰來參加聚會好呢？

▶ **Should** we bring our laptops along? 我們要帶我們的筆記型電腦來嗎？

▶ I asked him which one I **should** buy. 我問他我該買那一個。

▶ He asked me if he **should** leave a message. 他問我他是否該留言。

(e) 助動詞 shall 在直述句中與第二、三人稱連用時，可以表示「決心」、「承諾」、「警告」、「規定」、「命令」或「勸諫」等意。

USAGE PRACTICE

▶ He **shall** do as he likes! 他會按照他喜歡的方式去做！（決心）

▶ You **shall** have this pen back tomorrow. 明天一定把這支筆還你。（承諾）

▶ They **shall** be punished if they disobey my order.

如果他們不服從我的命令，他們將會被處罰。（警告）

▶ Visitors **shall** write down their names in this book. 參觀者要在這本書寫下名字。（規定）

▶ You **shall** go there with the message. 你一定要帶這個口信去那。（命令）

▶ You **shall not** tell lies, no matter how small they are.

你不應該說謊，不論是多麼小的謊言。（勸諫）

(f) 當助動詞 should 與完成式連用時，表示「應該做但未做的事」或加強「責備」或「惱怒」的語氣。

USAGE PRACTICE

▶ You **should** at least have told us that you were coming! 你至少應該告訴我們你要來！

▶ You **should** have helped him; he looked ill. 你當時應該幫他的；他看起來病了。

▶ You **should** have come with us. We had had a marvelous time!

你當時應該跟我們一起來的。我們玩得好愉快啊！

▶ You **should** have seen the film; it was really exciting!

你真應該看這部電影的；它真的很刺激！

▶ You **should** have told us what happened. 你當時應該告訴我們發生了什麼事。

(g) 助動詞 should 也常用來表示「義務」、「責任」或「應該」，此時相當於 ought to。

基礎文法寶典❹
Essential English Usage & Grammar

小練習

請在空格中填入助動詞 shall 或 should。

1. You _____ have told me the truth. You _____ not have lied to me.

2. I really don't know what I _____ have done if you hadn't come along at that moment.

3. I _____ do as I please; you have no right to order me about.

4. If you get good grades this term, I _____ buy you a new bicycle.

5. We _____ be waiting for you, so don't forget to come.

6. Where do you think I _____ hang this painting—over the television set or on this wall here?

7. We _____ have to report her to the police for stealing the wallet.

8. If I had been told the truth, I _____ not have behaved so badly.

9. The girls _____ have insisted that he _____ come to help them with their suitcases.

10. Terry _____ apologize to his cousin for playing tricks on her.

11. I don't know if I _____ go to the volleyball practice this afternoon.

12. I _____ do my best to complete the work if no one disturbs me.

13. We _____ be going for a ride in our new car tomorrow. If you behave yourself, we _____ let you join us.

13-6 will & would

(a) 助動詞 will 可以與原形動詞構成未來式。

▶ We **will** be waiting for you there. 我們會在那裡等你。(未來進行式)

▶ The tailor **will** have sewn the dress by then.

到那時，裁縫師將已經縫製好這件洋裝了。(未來完成式)

▶ She **will** have gone by the time you reach there.

你們到達那時，她將已經離去。(未來完成式)

(b) would 則是 will 的過去式。

USAGE PRACTICE

▶ I said that I **would** go with you. 我說我會和你一起去。

▶ He said that he **would** come today. 他說他今天會來。

▶ She hoped that the rowdy boys **would** have gone by then.

她希望這些喧鬧的男孩到時會已經離開了。

▶ We were hoping that they **would** be here in time for the concert.

我們一直希望他們會及時來這裡聽音樂會。

▶ I told her that I **would** not be seeing her again. 我告訴她我不會和她再見面了。

▶ He knew that I **would** be unable to come. 他知道我會無法前來。

▶ I asked him if he **would** tell me about it later. 我問他是否稍後會告訴我這件事。

 注意 will 或 would 可和 not 縮寫成一個字，例如 will not 寫成 won't、would not 寫成 wouldn't。

(c) 助動詞 will 和 would 可以在條件句中使用：will 多用於真實條件句；would 與原形動詞可以構成「與現在事實相反」的假設語氣，而與完成式可以構成「與過去事實相反」的假設語氣。

USAGE PRACTICE

▶ He **will** be angry if I don't go. 如果我不去，他會生氣。

▶ If we miss the bus, we **will** be late. 如果我們錯過這班公車，我們就會遲到。

▶ If you don't apologize, I **will not** give it back to you. 如果你不道歉，我不會把它還給你。

▶ If he resists, they **will** knock him out. 如果他抵抗，他們會擊倒他。

▶ I **would** do it if I could. 如果我可以，我會做這事。(與現在事實相反的假設語氣)

▶ If he fought them, he **would** be killed.

如果他跟他們作戰，他將會被殺死。（與現在事實相反的假設語氣）

▶ If he had been here, he **would** have created a lot of trouble.

如果他當時在這裡，他會製造許多麻煩。（與過去事實相反的假設語氣）

▶ If I had asked him, he **would** have agreed at once.

如果我當時向他請求，他會立刻同意。（與過去事實相反的假設語氣）

▶ We **would** have been very late if it had not been for that kind driver.

要不是有那個好心的司機，我們本來會遲到很久的。（與過去事實相反的假設語氣）

▶ It **would** have fallen on the floor if that man had not caught it in time.

如果那男人沒有及時接住它的話，它本來會掉到地上。（與過去事實相反的假設語氣）

▶ If she had listened to us, she **wouldn't** have been in this trouble.

如果她當時聽我們的話，她就不會惹上這個麻煩。（與過去事實相反的假設語氣）

(d) 在疑問句中，助動詞 will 可表示「請求」或「邀請」，既使在現在式中也可用 would，表示「更客氣的請求」。

USAGE PRACTICE

▶ **Will** you come to my house tomorrow?　明天來我家嗎？

▶ **Will** you do this for me?　你要幫我做這件事嗎？

▶ **Would** you please hand me that box?　請把那個盒子遞給我好嗎？

▶ **Would** you help me, please?　請幫我好嗎？

▶ **Would** you like to have another piece of cake?　再吃一塊蛋糕好嗎？

▶ "**Would** you like to stay for dinner?" she asked him.　「留下來吃晚餐好嗎？」她問他。

(e) 助動詞 will 可以用來表示「現在習慣性的動作」，而 would 則可以表示「過去習慣性的動作」。

USAGE PRACTICE

▶ She **will** come to me whenever she is in trouble.　每當她處於困境時，她都會來找我幫忙。

▶ They **will** always talk about politics at these meetings.　在這些會議中，他們總會討論政治。

▶ The dog **will** bark when it sees us.　當這隻狗看見我們時，牠都會吠叫。

▶ Mrs. Hill **will** bake cakes whenever we visit her.

每當我們去看希爾太太的時候，她都會烤蛋糕。

▶ He **would** go for long walks in the evenings. 過去他晚上都會散步很久。

▶ My mother **would** always make hot pancakes whenever it rained heavily.

以前每當下大雨時，我媽總會做熱騰騰的煎餅。

▶ The old soldier **would** tell them stories about the war.

老兵過去都會告訴他們關於戰爭的故事。

(f) 助動詞 would 可用在 wish 或 if only 之後的子句中，表達「願望」或「盼望」之意。

USAGE PRACTICE

▶ I wish she **would** come back quickly. 我希望她會很快回來。

▶ If only they **would** bring us something to eat! 但願他們會給我們帶來吃的東西！

▶ If only he **would** stop grumbling! 但願他會停止發牢騷！

▶ I wish that you **would** not be so noisy. 我希望你不會如此吵鬧。

▶ I wish that she **would** stop yawning. 我希望她會停止打呵欠。

(g) 助動詞 will 可以表示「強烈的意志」，用來加強語氣。would 則表示過去的強烈意志。

USAGE PRACTICE

▶ I **will** go anywhere I like. 我會去我喜歡去的任何地方。

▶ I **will** approach the stranger myself. 我將親自接近那個陌生人。

▶ We **will** have our say! 我們會說我們想說的話！

▶ We **will** do it without their help. 沒有他們的幫助，我們也會做這件事。

▶ She **will** go out in the rain despite my objections. 儘管我反對，她還是會在下雨時出門。

▶ They **will** take it without our permission. 沒有我們的許可，他們還是會拿走它。

▶ They **would** bring their muddy boots into the house! 他們還是把泥濘的靴子穿進房子裡！

▶ She **would** slam the door. 她還是很用力地關門。

(h) 助動詞 will 可以表示「希望他人遵守的正式命令或聲明」。

USAGE PRACTICE

▶ No one **will** step out of here without permission. 沒有許可，任何人都不能走出這裡。

▶ You **will** pick up all the papers that you scattered on the floor.

你必須撿起所有你散落在地上的報紙。

▶ You **will** stay behind and clean up the mess. 你要留下，清理這一團髒亂。

▶ You **will** not leave until I say so. 直到我叫你離開，你才能離開。

▶ School **will** close three days from now on. 從現在起學校將關閉三天。

▶ Shopping hours **will** be extended to 10 p.m. 購物時間將延長到晚上十點。

請在空格中填入助動詞 will 或 would。

1. If he had not come here, I _____ have gone to his house.

2. I wanted to know if she _____ lend me her book on flower decoration.

3. _____ you please tell him to return the garden tools he borrowed last week?

4. Those children _____ smile and wave at you whenever you pass their house.

5. If you find the notebook I lost yesterday, _____ you please return it to me?

6. I am very sorry about this mistake. It _____ not happen again; I promise you.

7. I wish he _____ not keep on pestering me to go to the movies with him.

8. She _____ sit in a corner and daydream whenever she came here for a visit.

9. "_____ you please inform her that I _____ not be able to go to her house this evening?" he said.

10. At that moment, I was hoping the earth _____ open and swallow me up!

11. It is such a boring day. I wish something exciting _____ happen around here.

12. He _____ be free from nine to nine-thirty. You should come at that time.

13. My brother _____ be leaving for England soon. He _____ be studying law there.

14. She _____ be annoyed if I told her about this matter. She _____ also be angry if I didn't.

☞ 更多相關習題請見本章應用練習 Part 12～Part 15。

13-7 can & could

(a) 助動詞 can 可以用來表示「做某事的能力或才能」，過去式則是 could。

USAGE PRACTICE

▶ He **can** cook a meal by himself. 他能獨自做一餐。

▶ She **can** speak three languages. 她會說三種語言。

▶ I **can** beat him in swimming anytime! 我隨時都能在游泳方面擊敗他!

▶ They **can't** play the guitar well. 他們不太會彈吉他。

▶ She **can't** sing because she has a sore throat. 她因為喉嚨痛而無法唱歌。

▶ He **can't** bear the smell of smoke. 他無法忍受煙味。

▶ She **could** paint very well before her accident. 出意外前,她能畫一手好畫。

▶ He **could** walk when he was only eight months old. 當他只有八個月大時,他就會走路了。

▶ I **couldn't** say a single word. 我一個字也說不出來。

 can 或 could 可和 not 縮寫成一個字,例如 can not 寫成 can't(另外還有一種比較正式的形式 cannot)、could not 寫成 couldn't。

(b) 在完成式或未來式中,用 be able to 代替助動詞 can。

USAGE PRACTICE

▶ She **has** been able to repay all her debts. 她已經能夠付清所有的債務了。

▶ You **will** be able to drive after a few more lessons. 再過幾堂課後,你就會開車了。

 對於過去的動作,不一定總是使用 could;當表示「經由某些努力達成的事情」時,也會以 was/were able to 代替助動詞 could。

▶ She finished her work early, so she **was able to** attend the concert.
她很早做完工作,所以能去參加音樂會。

▶ She **was able to** swim only half the length of the pool before she gave up.
在她放棄之前,她只能游完游泳池的一半距離。

▶ I **was able to** pass the examination because I worked hard. 我能通過考試,因為我努力讀書。

▶ He **was not able to** walk until a year after his operation. 直到手術一年後,他才能走路。

(c) 助動詞 can 或 could 也可以用來表示「許可」或「請求許可」。

USAGE PRACTICE

▶ You **can** leave now if you have finished the work.
如果你已完成這工作,你現在就可以離去。

▶ The professor says that we **can** sit for the examination.
教授說我們可以參加這個考試。

基礎文法寶典❹
Essential English Usage & Grammar

▶ She **can** go to the movies with her friends if she wants to.

如果她想的話，她可以和她朋友去看電影。

▶ We **can** rest here without being disturbed. 我們可以在這裡休息，不被打擾。

 依此延伸，否定型態的 can't 或 couldn't 可以表示「禁止」或「不准許」。

▶ You **can't** say such a thing without any proof. 沒有證據，你不可以這樣的說話。

▶ He **couldn't** enter the country because he had no visa. 因為他沒有簽證，他不可進入這個國家。

(d) 助動詞 can 或 could 也可以用來表示「可能性」。

USAGE PRACTICE

▶ The night temperature in the Sunridge Highlands **can** be quite low.

桑瑞吉高地夜晚的氣溫可能很低。

▶ Working under pressure **could** lead to a mental breakdown.

工作壓力可能會導致精神崩潰。

 依此延伸，否定型態的 can't 或 couldn't 可以表示「實際上不可能」。

▶ Surely he **can't** be strong enough! 當然，他不可能夠強壯！

▶ The house looks so deserted; there **can't** be anybody living in it.

這房子看起來廢棄很久了；不可能有人住在裡面。

▶ There are no lights on; they **can't** be at home. 沒有燈開著；他們不可能在家。

▶ He was far away when the robbery took place, so he **couldn't** have been involved.

當搶案發生時，他在很遠的地方，所以他不可能涉案。

(e) 助動詞 can 或 could 也可以用來表示「不相信」或「懷疑」。

USAGE PRACTICE

▶ **Can** he do it? 他會做嗎？

▶ **Can** he be telling the truth after all? 他究竟有可能說實話嗎？

▶ His story **could** be true, but it does sound absurd.

他的故事可能是真的，但是聽起來很荒謬。

▶ He **couldn't** be their father; he is too young. 他不可能是他們的父親；他太年輕了。

(f) 助動詞 could 可以用來表達「客氣的請求」。

▶ **Could** I have some more coffee, please? 我可以再要一些咖啡嗎？

▶ **Could** we come over for tea this afternoon? 我們今天下午可以過來喝茶嗎？

▶ **Could** I have a look at your new dictionary? 我能看一下你的新字典嗎？

▶ **Could** you lend me this book? 你能借我這本書嗎？

(g) 助動詞 can 常與無進行式型態的動詞連用。

▶ I **can** remember the day that we first met. 我可以記得我們初次見面的日子。

▶ He **can't** hear anything above the noise. 噪音讓他無法聽到其他任何聲音。

▶ I **can** smell something burning. 我可以聞到有東西著火了。

小練習

請在空格中填入助動詞 can 或 could（若需否定請用縮寫形式）。

1. She _____ walk before she was a year old.

2. We thought he _____ carry that box, but we were wrong.

3. You _____ come with me to the show if you like.

4. He _____ attend the meeting today because he is ill.

5. She _____ get tickets as there was already a long line at the movie theater.

6. We _____ see anything in the dark, _____ you?

7. You _____ sell your car if you put an advertisement in the newspaper.

8. She _____ see better now that she has got her glasses.

9. He borrowed an axe so that he _____ cut the tree down.

10. The plane _____ reach its destination on schedule owing to the bad weather.

11. He has saved up enough money. Now, he _____ go to Europe for a holiday.

12. "_____ you type at a speed of forty words per minute?" "No, I _____."

13. They _____ have escaped through the back door as it was not locked.

14. The rain has stopped. We _____ go home now.

☞ 更多相關習題請見本章應用練習 Part 16～Part 19。

13-8 may & might

(a) 助動詞 may 可以用來表示「許可」或「請求許可」，比 can 或 could 更正式；may 的過去式是 might，而 might 用來表示「許可」時，語氣比 may 委婉。

USAGE PRACTICE

▶ You **may** go if you wish. 如果你想去，你就去吧。

▶ You **may** sit down over there. 你可以在那邊坐下。

▶ **May** I carry the bag for you? 我可以幫你拿手提袋嗎？

▶ **May** I go to Richard's house this evening? 今天晚上我可以去理查的家嗎？

▶ **May** we have our lunch at this restaurant? 我們可以在這家餐廳吃午餐嗎？

▶ "**May** I go now?" "Yes, you **may**." 「我現在可以離開了嗎？」「是的，你可以。」

▶ I said that I **might** stay here for a couple of days. 我說我可能會在這裡停留幾天。

▶ She said that she **might** come to the meeting tonight. 她說她今晚可以來開會。

▶ He wanted to know if he **might** put up for the night here. 他想知道是否能在這裡過夜。

▶ He asked if he **might** bring his pet mice along. 他問是否他可以帶他的寵物鼠一起來。

▶ They asked me if they **might** come to watch television. 他們問我是否他們可以來看電視。

(b) 助動詞 may 或 might 的否定式 may not 或 might not 則表示「不准」。

USAGE PRACTICE

▶ You **may not** walk on the grass. 你不可以踐踏草坪。

▶ She **may not** come here while you are studying. 當你正在唸書的時候，她不可以來這裡。

▶ "May I borrow your pen?" "No, you **may not**." 「我可以借用你的筆嗎？」「不，你不可以。」

▶ "May I sit on this chair?" "Yes, you may./No, you **may not**."

　「我可以坐在這椅子上嗎？」「是的，可以。／不，不可以。」

▶ The baby **might not** be given any fruit at night. 晚上不可餵這個嬰兒吃任何水果。

 注意 may 或 might 較少和 not 縮寫成一個字。might not 偶爾會寫成 mightn't，但 may not 寫成 mayn't 的情形很罕見。

(c) 助動詞 may 或 might 可以用來表示「對未來的推測」，但 might 的可能性比 may 小。

▶ I **may** refuse his offer to buy my bicycle. 我可能會拒絕他要買我的腳踏車的提議。

▶ You **may** be right; I don't know for sure. 你可能是對的；我不確定。

▶ You **may** win first prize. 你可能會贏得第一名。

▶ He **may** regret his decision later on. 他之後可能會後悔他的決定。

▶ We have a few minutes left; we **may** still catch the bus.

  我們還剩下幾分鐘；還可能趕上公車。

▶ I **might** go with you if I have the time. 如果我有時間，我可能會跟你一起去。

▶ Your plans **might** be ruined if you let her come along.

  如果你讓她一起來，你的計畫可能會泡湯。

▶ He **might** arrive in time, but I think that it's unlikely.

  他可能會及時到達，但是我想那不太可能。

▶ We just **might** meet her on the way. 我們剛好可能會在途中遇見她。

▶ She **might** not like the gift. 她可能不喜歡這個禮物。

(d) 助動詞 may 可以表示「祝福」或「願望」。

▶ **May** you have a safe voyage! 祝你旅途平安！

▶ **May** you have a pleasant journey. 祝你旅途愉快。

▶ **May** you enjoy long life! 祝你長命百歲！

▶ **May** you always be happy! 祝你永遠快樂！

▶ **May** he pass the examination. 願他通過考試。

▶ **May** they continue to enjoy good health. 願他們永保健康。

▶ **May** God bless you! 願上帝保佑你！

(e) 助動詞 may 與完成式連用時，可以表示「對過去的推測」；might 表達的可能性比 may 小。

▶ "Brenda is late." "She **may** have missed the bus, or she **may** have been delayed."

  「布蘭達遲到了。」「她可能錯過公車，或是可能被耽誤了。」

▶ She isn't here; she **may** have gone to Mary's house.　她不在這裡；她可能已經去瑪麗家了。

▶ She **might** have gone shopping although she doesn't have much money.

　　雖然她沒有很多錢，但她可能已經去購物了。

▶ He **might** have sold the house, but I have not heard anything about the sale.

　　他可能已經出售房子了，但是我還沒聽說任何有關買賣的消息。

(f) 助動詞 may 和 might 也可以用在條件句：may 多用於真實條件句；might 加上原形動詞可以用來表示「與現在事實相反」的假設語氣，might 加上完成式可以用來表示「與過去事實相反」的假設語氣。

USAGE PRACTICE

▶ If he shouts, you **may** gag him.　如果他大吼，你可以塞住他的嘴巴。

▶ If the baby cries, you **may** feed him.　如果嬰兒哭了，你可以餵他。

▶ If you asked me, I **might** lend it to you.

　　如果你問我，我可能會借給你。（與現在事實相反的假設語氣）

▶ If he ran faster, he **might** win the race.

　　如果他跑得快點，他可能會贏得比賽。（與現在事實相反的假設語氣）

▶ They **might** pass if they studied hard enough.

　　如果他們讀書夠努力，就可能及格。（與現在事實相反的假設語氣）

▶ If it had not been for the lifeguard, she **might** have drowned.

　　如果不是那位救生員，她可能早就溺死了。（與過去事實相反的假設語氣）

▶ If you hadn't told me, I **might not** have known.

　　如果你沒有告訴我，我可能不會知道。（與過去事實相反的假設語氣）

(g) 助動詞 may 和 might 也可以用於表示「讓步」和「目的」的副詞子句。

USAGE PRACTICE

▶ It **may** be noon, but it's cold.　既使現在是中午，但是仍然很冷。

▶ Hard as they **might** try, they couldn't move the huge rock.

　　他們雖然盡力嘗試，但仍然無法移動這塊巨石。

▶ He **might** be rich, but he isn't very happy.　他可能很富有，但他不是很快樂。

▶ Lift the child up so that he **may** see the Lion Dance.　把孩子抱高一點，讓他能看到舞獅。

▶ We study Japanese so that we **might** be fluent in it. 我們學日文，以便能夠流暢地使用它。

▶ He works so that he **may** support himself. 他工作，以便能養活自己。

 在表示「目的」的副詞子句中，can 比 may 更常用。

(h) 助動詞 may 和 might 可以用來表示「比較委婉的命令或責備」。表示「命令」時，may 通常用在正式公告中；表示「責備」時，一般都使用 might。

USAGE PRACTICE

▶ Participants **may** not enter the room until the bell rings.

參賽者直到鈴響才可以進入房間裡。（命令）

▶ They **might** at least have thanked us! 他們至少應該感謝我們吧！（責備）

▶ You **might** have offered to help. 你至少應該幫個忙吧。（責備）

請在空格中填入助動詞 may 或 might。

1. You _____ apply for citizenship after staying in that country for ten years.

2. The flowers _____ fade if she doesn't put them in water.

3. He _____ have called while I was away.

4. "_____ I switch on the lights?" "No, you _____ not."

5. We thought that it _____ be the right answer after all.

6. The boys _____ have forgotten all about it if I hadn't reminded them.

7. My parents _____ not have allowed me to go if you hadn't come along.

8. If he isn't operated on in time, the disease _____ spread to other parts of the body. He _____ even die within the year.

9. They asked her if they _____ use the badminton court for their practice.

10. My brother _____ go overseas next year for further studies.

11. You _____ not use my razor to sharpen your pencils.

12. The soldiers _____ be having their annual parade in town this week. _____ we go to watch them?

13. The thief _____ have climbed into the room through the roof.

14. He _____ not succeed if he doesn't try harder.

☞ 更多相關習題請見本章應用練習 Part 20～Part 22。

13-9 must

(a) 助動詞 must 可以用來表示「義務」、「勸戒」或「命令」。

USAGE PRACTICE

▶ You **must** always wash your hands before a meal. 吃飯前，你一定都要洗手。

▶ You **must** stay here. 你必須留在這裡。

▶ You **must** do what I tell you. 你必須照我告訴你的去做。

▶ We **must** use this route. 我們必須走這條路線。

▶ She **must** finish her work by tomorrow. 明天前，她必須完成她的工作。

▶ He **must** go home early. 他必須早點回家。

▶ They **must** be on time for the rehearsal. 他們必須準時來排演。

---

 must 只有原形，不用在過去式和未來式，若要表示這兩個時態，必須使用 have to。have to 在大部分的情況中都可以取代 must。have to 裡的 have 是普通動詞，所以否定式要用 don't/doesn't/didn't have to。

▶ I **have to** learn to cook. 我必須學會烹飪。

▶ We **have to** eat in order to live. 為了生存，我們必須進食。

▶ You **have to** pay attention to the lesson. 你必須注意這門課。

▶ You **have to** respect your superiors. 你必須尊敬你的前輩。

▶ You **have to** do this; it's a rule. 你必須做這件事；這是規定。

▶ They **have to** use this bridge to go over. 他們必須用這座橋過去。

▶ Everyone **has to** obey these orders. 每一個人都必須服從這些命令。

▶ She **has to** leave early to catch the train. 她必須提早離開去趕火車。

▶ He **has to** go home early. 他必須早點回家。

▶ We don't **have to** go to the dentist again. 我們不需要再去看牙醫。

▶ I **had to** go to the doctor yesterday. 昨天我必須去看醫生。

▶ I **had to** wait until they were ready. 我必須等到他們準備好。

▶ He **had to** stay behind as punishment. 他必須留下作為處罰。

▶ You'll **have to** tell her the truth. 你將必須告訴她真相。

▶ He will **have to** go to Bangkok tomorrow. 他明天將必須去曼谷。

▶ They will **have to** be on time for the rehearsal. 他們將必須準時排演。

▶ We will **have to** stay with Grandpa during the holidays. 我們在假期期間將得和爺爺住在一起。

▶ I will **have to** move all this furniture to the new house. 我將必須把所有傢俱搬到新家去。

(b) must not（可縮寫為 mustn't）表示「禁止」。

USAGE PRACTICE

▶ She **must not** know that we are here. 不可以讓她知道我們在這裡。

▶ We **mustn't** let anyone know about it. 我們不可以讓任何人知道有關它的事情。

▶ You **must not** do that again. 你不可以再那麼做了。

(c) 助動詞 must 也可以表示「對現在、過去或未來的肯定推測」。

USAGE PRACTICE

▶ He has been working hard all day; he **must** be tired. 他整天一直努力工作；他一定很疲倦了。

▶ The lights are on; they **must** be home already. 電燈亮著；他們一定已經在家了。

▶ She **must** have received my letter. I sent it three days ago.

她一定已經收到我的信了，我在三天前寄出的。

▶ He looks sleepy; he **must** have been working all night.

他看起來很睏；他一定整夜都在工作。

小練習

請在空格中填入助動詞 must（過去式或未來式的情況則用 have to 取代）。

1. They _____ climb the stairs quietly as the baby was asleep.

2. All of you _____ stand at attention as soon as the band plays the national anthem.

3. You _____ wash your hands before you eat.

4. She _____ wear her glasses all the time as she cannot see without them.

5. When we arrived, they were not ready yet, so we _____ wait.

6. I _____ return the books to him next Saturday.

7. You _____ swim very well to win the competition this afternoon.

8. The school bus did not come, so we _____ walk.

9. You _____ not do a thing like that. You _____ apologize to her tomorrow.

10. I _____ go to the dentist now. I _____ not delay my appointment any longer.

11. We _____ work hard in order to pass the coming examinations.

基礎文法寶典❹
Essential English Usage & Grammar

12. The students were told that they _____ write more neatly.

13. He has worked hard all day; he _____ be tired.

14. The old man had a relapse, so he _____ be admitted to the hospital.

☞ 更多相關習題請見本章應用練習 Part 23～Part 26。

13-10 ought to

(a) 助動詞 ought to 表示「應該做某事的責任或義務」，ought to 的語氣比 should 強，但比 must 和 have to 弱。ought to 不必依人稱或時態而做變化。

USAGE PRACTICE

▶ You **ought to** behave yourself. 你應該要乖一點。

▶ You **ought to** clean the blackboard; it is very dirty. 你應該把黑板擦乾淨；它很髒了。

▶ He **ought to** pay for what he has bought. 他應該為他買的東西付錢。

▶ They **ought to** look after the little boy properly. 他們應該妥善照顧那個小男孩。

▶ They **ought to** be more polite. 他們應該更有禮貌。

(b) 在否定句中，should not 比 ought not to（可縮寫成 oughtn't to）常用；在疑問句中通常也會用 should，較少用 ought to 開頭。

USAGE PRACTICE

▶ You **shouldn't** run across the street. 你不應該跑到對街去。（較常用）

▶ You **oughtn't** to run across the street. 你不應該跑到對街去。（不常用）

▶ **Should** you wait here? 你應該在這裡等嗎？（較常用）

▶ **Ought** you **to** wait here? 你應該在這裡等嗎。（不常用）

▶ She **ought not to** water the plants so often. 她不應該如此常給植物澆水。（不常用）

▶ You **ought not to** eat so much; you are getting fat.
你不該吃這麼多；你會變胖的。（不常用）

▶ **Ought** she **to** tell the police about the threat? 她應該告訴警察她被恐嚇了嗎？（不常用）

▶ **Ought** I **to** go to help them? 我應該去幫他們嗎？（不常用）

▶ **Ought** we **to** tell them, or will you do it? 該由我們告訴他們，還是由你去做呢？（不常用）

(c) ought to 也可以表示「可能性」。

▶ I **ought to** be there within an hour. 一個小時之內我應該就會到那裡。

▶ If he left at six, he **ought to** be home by now. 如果他六點離開,他現在應該到家了。

▶ He **ought to** arrive anytime now. 他現在應該隨時會到。

▶ They **ought to** be back soon. 他們應該很快就會回來。

▶ The cake **ought to** be baked by now. 蛋糕現在應該在烤了。

(d) ought to 也可以表示「忠告」。

▶ You **ought to** think before you speak. 說話之前,你應該先想想。

▶ You **ought to** cut your hair shorter. 你應該把你的頭髮剪短一點。

▶ You **ought to** visit that place; it's a shopper's paradise.

你應該參觀那個地方,它是一個購物天堂。

▶ You **ought to** tidy up your room. It is very messy.

你應該把你的房間收拾整齊,它實在很亂。

▶ He has to walk a long way to school. You **ought to** give him a ride.

他必須走一大段路去上學,你應該載他去。

▶ She **ought to** boil the water before putting in the tea leaves.

在放進茶葉之前,她應該先把水煮沸。

▶ She **ought to** see a doctor before her cough becomes worse.

在她的咳嗽變得更嚴重之前,她應該先去看醫生。

(e) 助動詞 ought to 及 should 可以指「現在或未來的責任」。

▶ They **ought to/should** clean the rooms now. 他們現在應該清理房間了。

▶ She **ought to/should** go home tomorrow. 她明天應該回家去。

(f) 助動詞 ought to 及 should 接完成式構成「與過去事實相反」的假設語氣,表示「過去應該做而未做的事」。

基礎文法寶典❹
Essential English Usage & Grammar

▶ They **ought to/should** have locked the door last night. 他們昨晚應該把門鎖上的。

▶ You **should** have seen his face! He looked so comical.

  你當時真應該看看他的臉！他看起來是如此滑稽。

▶ You **ought to** have taken the teacher's advice. 你當時應該接受老師的忠告。

▶ You **ought not to** have spent all your pocket money! 你當時不應該花光你的零用錢的！

▶ You **oughtn't to** have chased it away. 你當時不應該把牠嚇跑的。

▶ You **ought to** have been more polite to them. 你當時應該對他們更有禮貌。

▶ You **shouldn't** have made so much noise. You have awakened the baby.

  你不該那麼吵鬧，你已經把寶寶吵醒了。

▶ You **ought not to** have told them about it. 你當時不應該把那件事告訴他們的。

▶ She **ought to/should** have fed the cat yesterday. 她昨天應該餵貓的。

▶ She **ought to** have arrived punctually. 她當時應該準時到達的。

▶ She **shouldn't** have been so rude! 她當時不應該那麼粗魯！

▶ They **should** have listened to me. Then, they wouldn't have got into such trouble.

  他們當初應該聽我的話，那麼他們就不會陷入這樣的麻煩。

 小練習

請利用 "ought to + 完成式" 的結構改寫句子（時間副詞或片語一律置於句尾）。

1. The gardener should burn the rubbish. (*this morning*)

  → _____

2. You ought not to drive so fast. (*last night*)

  → _____

3. She should take an umbrella along. (*just now*)

  → _____

4. He should follow the instructions. (*two days ago*)

  → _____

5. The farmers should buy modern machinery with their government loans. (*last year*)

  → _____

6. It's going to rain. You should not put the clothes out to dry. (*just now*)

  → _____

7. The chicken coop ought to be washed. (*early this morning*)

→ _____

8. He shouldn't break that promise. (*last week*)

→ _____

9. The student should be punished for the theft. (*immediately*)

→ _____

10. The match ought to start. (*at five o'clock*)

→ _____

11. They should cut down the tree. (*a month ago*)

→ _____

12. He ought to write to his uncle. (*last Friday*)

→ _____

13. You shouldn't be so careless. (*yesterday*)

→ _____

14. She ought to leave them alone. (*last night*)

→ _____

13-11 need

(a) 助動詞 need 主要用於否定句及疑問句，在肯定句中 need 則是當一般動詞使用。
助動詞 need 不必依人稱而變化，否定要用 need not（或縮寫為 needn't）。

USAGE PRACTICE

▶ You **need not** go if you don't want to. 如果你不想的話，你沒有必要去。

▶ She **needn't** have torn the letter. 她沒有必要撕掉那封信。

▶ I **needn't** go to the library today. 今天我不需要去圖書館。

▶ We **need not** change our clothes. 我們不需要換衣服。

▶ **Need** everyone turn up for the rehearsal? 每一個人都必須來排演嗎？

▶ **Need** he have beaten the dog so severely? 他需要這麼嚴厲地打那隻狗嗎？

▶ **Need** we bring all our books? 我們有必要把全部的書都帶來嗎？

▶ "**Need** we paint the room today?" "No, we needn't."

「今天我們必須油漆這個房間嗎？」「不，我們不必。」

現代美語已經很少將 need 當作助動詞使用，建議不管是肯定句、否定句或疑問句，請都把 need 視為一般動詞。

▶ I **needed** a clean page. 我需要乾淨的一頁紙。

▶ He **needs** some exercise. 他需要做一些運動。

▶ He **needs** a rest. 他需要休息。

▶ She doesn't **need** the light. 她不需要燈。

▶ We didn't **need** the torch at all. 我們一點也不需要火把。

▶ Do you **need** a clean shirt? 你需要一件乾淨的襯衫嗎？

(b) need not 可以作 must 的否定式，表示「沒有做某事的必要或義務」。

USAGE PRACTICE	
▶ I **must** clean the window. 我必須清洗窗戶。	→ I **need not** clean it. 我不必清洗它。
▶ We **must** rent a room. 我們必須租一個房間。	→ We **need not** rent one. 我們不必租。
▶ She **must** get some help. 她必須找人幫忙。	→ She **needn't** get any help. 她不必找人幫忙。

 勿將 need not 與 must not 混淆。need not 表示「不需要」，而 must not 則表示「禁止」。

▶ You **needn't** go up to wake her. She is up already. 你不需要去叫醒她，她已經起床了。

▶ You **mustn't** go up to wake her. She won't like it. 你不可以去叫醒她，她會不高興的。

▶ You **need not** come here again. 你不需要再來這裡了。

▶ You **must not** come here again. 你不可以再來這裡了。

▶ He **need not** go there. 他不需要去那裡。

▶ He **must not** go there. 他不可以去那裡。

▶ You **must not** leave the house. 你不准離開這房子。

▶ We **must not** steal. 我們不可以偷東西。

▶ The soup is salty enough; I **needn't** add any more salt. 湯夠鹹了；我不需要再加鹽。

▶ You **need not** do the dishes. 你不需要洗碗。

▶ You **need not** come. We have enough people to help us.
你不需要來，我們有足夠的人手幫我們。

▶ He **needn't** come for practice since he is not on the team. 因為他不是隊員，他不需要來練習。

▶ We **needn't** ask for his help. 我們不需要請他幫忙。

▶ We **needn't** hurry. There is still plenty of time. 我們不需要急，時間還很多。

請在空格中填入助動詞 needn't 或 mustn't。

1. You _____ talk so loudly. The baby is asleep.

2. You _____ laugh; it's not funny!

3. It is raining; you _____ water the plants today.

4. We _____ stay too long. It's getting dark.

5. You _____ go out by yourself at night. It is too dangerous.

6. The essay is neatly written. You _____ rewrite it.

7. You _____ throw rubbish everywhere.

8. Tell him that he _____ take the book home. It is not allowed.

9. You _____ get up early. The car will not come until half past ten.

10. You _____ shout. I can hear you perfectly.

11. He _____ try to be polite. I do not like him at all.

12. We _____ drive too fast on a rainy day.

13. We _____ make any noise or else the teacher will punish us!

14. You _____ come for practice tomorrow. You may stay home and rest.

15. What is done is done. You _____ upset yourself.

16. "What has been said in this room _____ be repeated. Do you understand?"

☞ 更多相關習題請見本章應用練習 Part 27～Part 28。

13-12 dare & used to

(a) dare 可以當作助動詞或一般動詞使用。當助動詞時，dare 不依人稱而變化，且後接原形動詞。否定要用 dare not（或縮寫為 daren't）。當一般動詞時，後面可以接不定詞，再接原形動詞。

USAGE PRACTICE

▶ He **dares** to climb the tree. 他敢爬樹。（一般動詞）

▶ **Dare** he climb the tree? 他敢爬樹嗎？（助動詞）

▶ I **dared** him to fight. 我激他打架。（一般動詞）

▶ You **dare not** fight. 你不敢打架。（助動詞）

▶ Don't you **dare** to touch it! 你敢碰它！（一般動詞）

▶ How **dare** you touch it! 你怎麼敢碰它！（助動詞）

基礎文法寶典❹
Essential English Usage & Grammar

▶ He **dared** to touch it although I told him not to.

雖然我告訴他不行，但是他還是敢碰它。（一般動詞）

▶ She **won't dare** to go alone. 她不會敢單獨去。（一般動詞）

(b) 助動詞 dare 較常用於否定句和疑問句中。

USAGE PRACTICE

▶ **Dare** he light the firecracker? 他敢點燃爆竹嗎？

▶ She **daren't** go there, **dare** she? 她不敢去那裡，是嗎？

 助動詞 dare 的慣用語 "I dare say..." 表示「（我想）大概、可能…」。

▶ She has not arrived yet, but **I dare say** she will come eventually.

她還沒到，但是我想她大概最後還是會來。

▶ This masterpiece of yours will fetch a high price, **I dare say**. 我想你的傑作大概會賣得好價錢。

▶ **I dare say** it will rain this afternoon. 我想今天下午可能會下雨。

(c) 助動詞 used to 沒有現在式或未來式的形式，可以用來表示「沒有持續到現在的過去習慣」。否定為 used not to，問句則是 "Used + 主詞 + to + 原形動詞 ...?" 的形式。

USAGE PRACTICE

▶ I **used to** play with marbles when I was young. 我小的時候，我常玩彈珠。

▶ We **used to** wade through that stream when we were children.

我們還是孩子的時候，我們常涉水過那條小溪。

▶ People **used to** think that the earth was the center of the universe.

人們以前認為地球是宇宙的中心。

▶ He **used to** travel by bus, but now he has bought a car.

他以前常搭公車旅行，但是現在他已經買車了。

▶ There **used to** be a well here. 這裡曾經有一口井。

▶ "**Used** he **to** be so short-tempered?" "No, he **used not to** lose his temper so quickly."

「他以前脾氣很壞嗎？」「不，他以前不常這麼容易發脾氣。」

▶ She **used not to** drink. 她以前不常喝酒。

實際上，現在美語已經不再將 used to 當作助動詞使用。請將 used 視為過去式的一般動詞，利用 didn't 構成否定句；利用 did 開頭構成問句。

▶ "**Did** he **use to** take a walk after dinner?" "No, he **didn't use to** do that."

「他以前習慣晚餐後要去散步嗎？」「不，他以前不常這樣。」

▶ She **didn't use to** make such a mistake, **did** she? 她以前不常犯過這樣的錯誤，有嗎？

(d) 勿將作助動詞用的 used to 和作形容詞用的 used 混淆。

USAGE PRACTICE

▶ He is **used** to getting up early in the morning. 他習慣早起。（形容詞）

▶ We **used to** wake up very early in those days.

在過去那些日子裡，我們常很早起床。（助動詞）

請在空格中填入助動詞 dare、ought to 或 used to，如句意有必要請改成否定。

1. The boy _____ be very hardworking, but now he's very lazy.

2. We _____ take long walks into the country long ago.

3. _____ he dive into the water from this height?

4. They _____ roam in the woods when they were young.

5. She's behaving very strangely. She _____ be very quiet, but now she's always making noise.

6. The postman _____ not deliver letters to our house because of our dog.

7. You _____ be so soft-hearted; people will take advantage of you.

8. This is where we _____ live. It's a very pretty place, isn't it?

9. He never _____ lose his temper so easily before.

10. This road _____ be resurfaced; it's in very bad condition.

11. "He _____ not even meet me, let alone fight me!" he taunted.

12. This man _____ be shut up in a cell; he is a public menace.

13. "How _____ you insult my sister!" Jack shouted.

14. "You _____ tell her the news, however bad it is." "I _____ not. She may have a complete breakdown."

15. There _____ be two rows of houses here, but they have been pulled down. The owners

基礎文法寶典❹
Essential English Usage & Grammar

_____ have been compensated for their loss, but they weren't.

☞ 更多相關習題請見本章應用練習 Part 29。

Chapter 13　應用練習

PART 1

請在空格中填入正確的現在式 be 動詞。

1. Nobody _____ willing to help organize the party, so it will be canceled.

2. There _____ someone knocking at the door.

3. Everyone present _____ expected to take part in the games.

4. There _____ enough water in the pot to make tea for all of us.

5. All the boys _____ ready to do as he says.

6. Those books on the shelf _____ to be dusted every day.

7. The pair of scissors _____ in the drawer of that cupboard.

8. How much of the money _____ left after paying for those things?

9. Time _____ valuable, so do not waste it.

10. There _____ something wrong with the sewing machine.

11. A lot of letters _____ sent by airmail to other countries.

12. None of the girls _____ in the house. Where have they gone?

13. There _____ a parade going down the street.

14. These _____ very expensive and hard to find.

15. The rest of the books I borrowed _____ still with me. I'll return them later.

16. _____ there enough seats for all of you?

17. The results of the contest _____ going to be announced a little while later.

18. The price of pineapples _____ lower here than anywhere else.

PART 2

請將下列句子改成否定句。

1. He has a cold now.

→ _____

2. We have taken the car to the garage.

→ _____

3. John has a dog named "Spot."

→ _____

4. The washerwoman has brought back the sheets.

→ _____

5. I have had my haircut.

→ _____

6. We have visitors staying with us at present.

→ _____

7. I am having difficulty completing the project. I have handed the job over to Mr. Hanson.

→ _____

8. The children had measles last year.

→ _____

9. She had broken her promise.

→ _____

10. They have the room cleaned daily.

→ _____

11. He has brown eyes and black hair.

→ _____

12. We had coffee at Jane's house just now.

→ _____

13. My aunt often has headaches.

→ _____

14. All the students have had inoculations against cholera.

→ _____

15. That hotel has a lot of tourists staying there.

→ _____

PART 3

請在空格中填入正確的 be 動詞或 have（若需否定請用縮寫形式），並注意必要的變化。

1. We _____ to meet him at the airport now.

2. His friend _____ here half an hour ago.

3. You _____ （請用否定）going now, _____ you?

4. _____ anyone seen my pencil sharpener?

5. Why _____ he angry with me now? What _____ I done to make him angry?

6. He _____ told me that he _____ to go for a medical examination.

7. He _____ waiting outside for you now. He _____ been there for half an hour.

8. He doesn't _____ the money with him now. He _____ going back to get it.

9. I usually _____ my dinner at seven-thirty, but yesterday I _____ it at nine.

10. "She _____ going to the party tonight, _____ （請用否定）she?" "No, she _____
（請用否定）."

11. _____ you going with her, too? If you _____, can I come along?

12. _____ （請用否定）these buildings supposed to be pulled down last year? They _____
so old that they look as if they _____ going to collapse any minute.

13. He often _____ headaches recently. His parents _____ told him to see a doctor, but
he _____ too afraid to go.

14. He _____ wearing overalls when she met him. He _____ black eyes; his hair
_____ curly and black, and he _____ no hat on.

15. He _____ （請用否定）coming today, either. He _____ supposed to come yesterday,
but it _____ raining heavily, so he _____ to postpone the trip.

PART 4

請在空格中填入一般動詞或助動詞 do（若需否定請用縮寫形式），並注意必要的變化。

1. I _____ not know what to do about this problem.

2. We _____ agree with you on this. What we _____ like is the way you present it.

3. I know everybody _____ such work, but I dislike it.

4. _____ she think she can come to my house tomorrow? If she _____, I won't wait for
her.

5. They _____ arrive quite early at the airport last night, _____ they?

6. "_____ that puppy belong to you?" "Oh, yes, it _____."

7. You _____ （請用否定）care if other people get hurt because of you, _____ you?

8. _____ open that box. If you _____, you will get a nasty shock.

9. Lucy _____ like being ordered about by any of her friends; neither _____ Janet.

10. I almost forget about it, but luckily I had noted it in my diary. So I _____, after all.

11. I _____ mind doing all the housework once in a while, but I _____ mind doing it every day.

12. "_____ you see anything?" "No, I _____. It's only your imagination."

13. "_____ floods often occur in this part of the country?" "Yes, they often _____."

14. I _____ often behave in such a silly way, but yesterday I _____, and now I'm so ashamed of what I've done.

PART 5

請在空格中填入一般動詞或助動詞 do（若需否定請用縮寫形式），並注意必要的變化。

1. I _____ hear what you said. Could you repeat it?

2. You like playing volleyball, _____ you?

3. She _____ come to your house as often as she used to, _____ she?

4. _____ they tell you that he had _____ this all by himself?

5. What _____ he _____ when he heard the news? _____ he get very angry?

6. "_____ you want to go with your uncle?" "No, I _____."

7. "We _____（請用否定）come too late last night, _____ we?" "No, you _____."

8. When _____ the rest of you want to complete it? _____ you want to _____ it now?

9. Are you _____ your homework now?

10. I _____ know what to _____ with these extra chairs. _____ you think I should keep them in the storeroom, or shall I sell them?

11. I hope he _____ break that window. If he _____, we will have to pay for it.

12. Julia usually cleans the kitchen, _____ she? I _____ think she has _____ it today; it is still dirty.

13. "Where _____ you get this penknife?" "You _____（請用否定）steal it, _____ you?" "No, I _____. I found it by the roadside."

14. I _____ agree with you, and neither _____ Peter. Sally is the only one here who _____ agree with you.

PART 6

請將下列句子改成問句，並做必要的變化。

1. They eat meat on Fridays.

   → _____

2. That baby cries for his milk every three hours.

   → _____

3. She missed the flight to Tokyo yesterday.

   → _____

4. Vincent plays golf every Saturday.

   → _____

5. The children behaved themselves very well yesterday.

   → _____

6. Somebody delivered the parcel to the house just now.

   → _____

7. He did very well in his mathematics test.

   → _____

8. The boys from next door always crawl through the hole in the fence.

   → _____

9. The principal presented him with a prize for being the best student of the year.

   → _____

10. The taxi went through the red light.

   → _____

11. He grumbles about his work.

   → _____

12. No one saw him being attacked.

   → _____

13. She usually leaves the house in a hurry in the morning.

   → _____

14. They spoke to the officer about the matter.

   → _____

15. I like three cubes of sugar in my coffee.

→ _____

16. It rains almost every afternoon.

→ _____

PART 7

請在空格中填入正確的 be 動詞或 do，並注意必要的變化。

1. He _____ say the most outrageous things yesterday, _____ he?

2. She _____ to play a part in the concert that will _____ held in the Town Hall next week, but she _____ not want to act at all.

3. Tabby, our cat, _____ very clean though she _____ not like to touch water.

4. The match will _____ held next Saturday. Those who want to practice may _____ so now.

5. My sisters _____ not understand French, but I _____ . That _____ why they _____ taking French lessons now.

6. Even though the policeman on the beat _____ keeping his eyes open for suspicious characters last night, he _____ not see the two strangers climbing the wall.

7. _____ you borrow a book from me? I _____ not know where I have put one of my books.

8. _____ not listen to him. If you _____ , you will be as bad as he _____ .

9. We _____ remind her yesterday, but she forgot again. She _____ a very forgetful person.

10. He _____ to catch the nine o'clock train, but he missed it.

11. "_____ stay for lunch," she urged. "We _____ having roast chicken today."

12. He _____ walking home one night when he saw a strange sight. He _____ not know whether to go nearer to look or run away.

13. I _____ asked to make an opening speech, but I declined as I _____ not know what to say.

14. "_____ quiet!" the prefect ordered. "If you _____ , you will be punished."

15. He _____ not want to join us, _____ he? If he _____ come along, we wouldn't have room for him in the car.

16. My brother _____ not wish to eat now; neither _____ I. We _____ not hungry

yet.

17. "I _____ going now. You _____ （請用否定） mind, _____ you?"

18. Lisa _____ to have waited for us at the movie theater, but she _____ nowhere to be seen when we arrived. Later, we found out that she _____ wait for us, but at another theater.

PART 8

請在空格中填入正確的 be 動詞或 do，並注意必要的變化。

1. _____ be lazy! You know that you've got to finish the work quickly, _____ you?

2. Be quiet, Peter! Your father _____ sleeping, so _____ make so much noise.

3. They _____ driving down to Rainbow Valley tomorrow, but they _____ know what time they will go.

4. _____ come again next week. I'll _____ expecting you on Saturday.

5. "What _____ you want? You _____ not supposed to come in here. Please go away at once," they implored.

6. The children _____ playing in the field last evening. They _____ hear their parents quarrelling.

7. She likes chocolates, _____ she? _____ ask her to take some more from the tray.

8. Those men _____ walking this way, _____ they? _____ you think that they will stop here?

9. You may not want to go, but I _____ . So, you _____ going to stay at home while I _____ going out.

10. "No one _____ to make any noise or try to run away. Do as you _____ told and no one will hurt you," the man said.

11. "_____ I have to take her along?" asked Sammy. "Yes, and _____ take care of her," said his mother.

12. He seldom loses his temper, but he _____ last night. I was terrified because he _____ look so fierce.

13. "_____ he know that you are here?" "No, he _____ . I _____ tell him."

14. I _____ know the answer, and neither _____ my brother. We _____ still trying to find it.

15. "Please _____ have another slice of cake. It _____ homemade. My daughter _____ always making cakes."

16. "_____ play with those matches! You _____ to return them to the kitchen drawer at once."

17. I _____ know the answer, but I _____ not going to tell you because you _____ supposed to work it out yourself.

18. "You may not be hungry, but we _____. Let's go out for dinner. Our stomachs _____ rumbling and grumbling!" they said.

PART 9

請在空格中填入正確的 be 動詞、do 或 have，並注意必要的變化（限用現在式）。

1. Everyone _____ gone to see the film that _____ showing in the Metro Cinema. Peter _____ not want to go because he _____ a toothache.

2. There _____ no one here who _____ qualified enough to do it. We'll _____ to get a specialist from the city.

3. My sister, who _____ nothing definite to do during the holidays, _____ accompanying me to Lakeside. I _____ already bought the train tickets.

4. Paul _____ not want to go to the party tomorrow, but his friends _____ trying to persuade him to change his mind.

5. Elizabeth, who _____ a seat at the far end of the room, _____ not like her place at all because she is nearsighted.

6. Some fishermen _____ gone out fishing in the storm. Their wives _____ waiting anxiously for them.

7. An accident _____ just occurred, but no one _____ injured. The parties involved have each gone their own way because they _____ not want to report it to the police.

8. "_____ come with us! We'll _____ a simply marvelous time together."

9. Those who _____ the time and _____ willing to help _____ been asked to come tomorrow. They do not _____ to bring anything.

10. She _____ not want to _____ anything to do with us because she says we _____ too rowdy.

11. There _____ many varieties of orchids; each _____ a beauty of its own.

12. There _____ a last-minute change in the plans that we _____ made.

13. The man who _____ selling insurance policies _____ gone around the whole neighborhood. Only a few _____ bought policies from him.

14. Molly _____ a large collection of CDs, but she _____ not played them for two days because her CD player _____ being repaired.

15. This book _____ useless now because many of its pages _____ missing. I _____ not know who _____ torn the pages out.

16. The police _____ set up roadblocks to catch a criminal who _____ still at large. No arrest _____ yet been made.

17. Those who _____ not possess a driving license _____ forbidden to drive. They will _____ to pay a fine if they _____ caught driving.

18. There _____ been an accident at the mine. A doctor _____ been called but there _____ little that he can do because the entrance to the mine _____ blocked.

19. She _____ not want to watch the ball game because the weather _____ too hot. She _____ found something else to do.

PART 10

請在空格中填入正確的 be 動詞、do 或 have，並注意必要的變化（限用現在式）。

1. We _____ not know what _____ happened to the girls. They _____ to meet us here, but they _____ not come so far.

2. "_____ you know the way to the police station?" "No, I _____ . I _____ not very familiar with this area."

3. It _____ getting late, and the boys _____ had a swim already. So, they _____ going home now.

4. John _____ a car, but he _____ not give a ride to anyone. He _____ always been rather possessive about his things.

5. They _____ not called us since last week. I wonder if something _____ happened to them. They _____ always so reckless!

6. It _____ grown dark already. They _____ to be here by six o'clock, but they _____ not come.

7. The girls _____ waiting for the bus. It _____ raining heavily and they _____

shivering.

8. Charles _____ changed a lot, _____ he? I _____ not suppose he wants to be our friend anymore.

9. The children _____ not feeling sleepy at all, so she lets them play for a while longer. When they _____ exhausted themselves, she will send them to bed.

10. I _____ no brothers or sisters, but I _____ a very good friend. He _____ in the same form as I.

11. It _____ getting late now. I _____ afraid that Ann _____ got no transportation home.

12. _____ visit us when you _____ in town again. We _____ always at home after five in the afternoon.

PART 11

請將下列句子改成否定句。

1. He has got a lot of detective novels in his room.

→ _____

2. She went out just now.

→ _____

3. They have all gone to church.

→ _____

4. He has a bath every morning before he goes to school.

→ _____

5. They need warm clothes for the winter there.

→ _____

6. The teacher has corrected all my essays.

→ _____

7. He had difficulty persuading her to go out with him.

→ _____

8. I have forgotten to bring my notes along.

→ _____

9. They submitted their application forms on the last day.

→ _____

10. He has got enough money to last him a lifetime.

→ _____

11. She has the windows washed every week.

→ _____

12. We have agreed to his suggestion. He explained it clearly to us last night.

→ _____

13. We had lost the game to the opposing team.

→ _____

14. She felt a moment's pity for the helpless creature.

→ _____

15. She asked the doctor about the condition of her grandfather.

→ _____

16. They have some friends staying for dinner tonight.

→ _____

PART 12

請在空格中填入助動詞 would 或 should。

1. You _____ not be so greedy, especially when you are in someone else's house.

2. I do wish they _____ come quickly. I am tired of all this waiting.

3. They left over an hour ago, so they _____ be back soon.

4. _____ you please switch on the fan? It is very hot here.

5. Knives _____ be kept away from the reach of children.

6. If you told him not to do it, he _____ deliberately do it.

7. They _____ let their son choose his own career, instead of forcing him to be a teacher.

8. _____ he call again, will you tell him that I do not want to talk to him?

9. I told her she _____ exercise more and eat less chocolate and less ice cream.

10. Something _____ be done about this disgusting state of affairs.

11. _____ you like some coffee, or _____ you prefer some lemonade?

12. The painting _____ look better on that wall, but it _____ take up too much space.

13. What _____ I do to make him listen to me? I _____ appreciate any advice from you.

14. _____ you mind letting me know the moment he arrives?

PART 13

請在空格中填入助動詞 would 或 should（若需否定請用縮寫形式）。

1. He said he _____ repair it for you without any payment, but I think that you _____ pay him.

2. She _____ have fallen down the slope if it hadn't been for that branch.

3. She _____ have been present. It was her duty to be there.

4. There _____ be no need for you to water the plants _____ it rain.

5. We asked them if they _____ help us, but they replied that they _____ .

6. It _____ be made known that this road _____ be closed to traffic next month.

7. There _____ be no necessity for you to panic. Help _____ arrive in time.

8. There _____ have been a 'Danger' sign here. If there had been one, the little girl _____ have fallen in.

9. You _____ have no trouble with this problem. It _____ be easy for you to solve.

10. If you _____ have any trouble with your work, I _____ be happy to help you out.

11. We _____ have done it for you if you had told us.

12. _____ there come a time when you need my help, I _____ gladly do so.

13. "I _____ worry if I were you. Enerything will be fine," I told the anxious woman.

14. You _____ at least have helped us to clean up the mess!

15. I knew that you _____ say that!

16. You _____ see a doctor about it; otherwise, your illness _____ get worse.

17. She _____ not have been saved if it had not been for that strong swimmer. She _____ be thankful to him.

18. We _____ have come if we had known that the swimming pool _____ be closed for repairs. We _____ have found that out before we came.

PART 14

請在空格中填入助動詞 would 或 should。

1. The cat _____ jump up on the bed and sleep at the foot of it.

2. You _____ get yourself a new pair of shoes if these are too tight.

3. _____ you mind opening the door? Here's the key.

4. If you _____ need any help, just call me and I _____ certainly come to your assistance.

5. I wish they _____ not play the music so loud. They _____ have enough sense to know that others are trying to sleep.

6. It's rather strange that he _____ return so early. Normally, he _____ stay out until past midnight.

7. Perhaps you _____ be kind enough to tell me where he has gone. If anybody _____ know, you're the one.

8. If the lady _____ come when I'm out, tell her I _____ be back by twelve.

9. The doctor told me that I _____ take a holiday. I _____ certainly like to, but I can't afford the time.

10. _____ the inspector ask you any questions, just say you don't know.

11. I _____ like to see the manager, please. He _____ have come back from lunch now.

12. It is absurd that he _____ think that way. I _____ not do such a monstrous thing!

13. If only it _____ stop pouring! We _____ have consulted the weather forecast for today.

14. "One _____ never lay the blame on others," his father said. "It _____ do you good to remember that."

15. The dog _____ wait at the doorstep for its master's return and _____ bark with joy when it heard the car.

16. I think you _____ park the car over there. It _____ be much safer.

17. If you _____ kindly wait for a few minutes, I _____ be able to find what you need among these files here.

18. "_____ you please put the instruments back after use? You _____ always remember that yourself without me to remind you," she said.

19. Where _____ I hide this box? If I left it in the room, he _____ definitely see it. It _____ be a place where he _____ not think of searching.

PART 15

請在空格中填入助動詞 would 或 should。

1. _____ you mind drawing the blinds?

2. She insisted that he _____ apologize.

3. _____ you please wait here while I see if Mr. Drake is in?

4. He took the one o'clock train, so he _____ be home by now.

5. _____ you be so good as to feed my dog while I'm away?

6. You _____ have stirred the mixture before you put it in the oven.

7. The cake _____ not have been so hard if you had added some more water.

8. It was decided that the case _____ be brought to court.

9. If the errand boy brings me a message while I'm not here, _____ you please accept it for me?

10. You _____ not leave the hospital before you're fully cured.

11. I wish the people upstairs _____ not stomp around so much. They _____ have some consideration for other people.

12. There's a good film at the Rex Cinema which you _____ see. _____ you come with me? I have an extra ticket.

13. I _____ not advise you to invest in this scheme. It's a very risky project.

14. He _____ be warned of the difficulties that he is going to encounter.

15. I _____ like to meet your friend. _____ I ask for a formal introduction?

16. He _____ not want to see you, so you _____ write to him instead of going to see him.

17. Don't you think you _____ consult your superior? He _____ tell you what to do.

18. I _____ not be far away. If anything _____ go wrong, don't hesitate to call me.

PART 16

請在空格中填入助動詞 can 或 could（若需否定請用縮寫形式）。

1. I _____ possibly finish the work and check through the figures in half an hour.

2. If he had informed me about it, I _____ have easily helped him.

3. "_____ we all go if Father agrees?" she asked.

4. None of us _____ do anything to help because they refused to let us go near.

5. They _____ watch television if they have nothing better to do.

6. He _____ play badminton last week because he twisted his wrist.

基礎文法寶典❹
Essential English Usage & Grammar

7. The train _____ pass because a tree had fallen across the rails.

8. You _____ mix the two colors to make green.

9. We _____ stop on the way for dinner if you want to.

10. If he managed to borrow a boat, we _____ go fishing.

11. If you _____ promise not to tell another person, I will let you in on the secret.

12. She didn't go shopping yesterday, so she _____ tell us what she bought.

13. The airplane _____ land because the strip of land is too small.

14. You _____ give him the message when he comes home.

15. I am sure they _____ lift the box by themselves.

16. If we paid for them, _____ we have front-row seats?

17. He took them to a place where nobody _____ find them.

18. The car _____ go further, for it had run out of petrol.

19. They _____ sing very well, _____ they? They just have the talent.

20. We _____ see very well because the light was dim.

PART 17

請在空格中填入助動詞 can 或 could（若需否定請用縮寫形式）。

1. She _____ have come here if she had wanted to.

2. Do you think that one of these boys _____ win the first prize?

3. He told us that we _____ go on the picnic if we had the money.

4. You _____ tell her that she _____ come with us if she wants to.

5. I _____ find my way out of that jungle and was trapped for three days.

6. If I had not missed the bus, I _____ have reached the movie theater on time.

7. They _____ recognize us because we were wearing masks.

8. In the past, people _____ travel easily from place to place, but now people _____ do so with ease.

9. You _____ come this way, but you certainly _____ go by that road because it is under repair.

10. You _____ eat as much as you like here, but you _____ take anything home.

11. I _____ remember her name at all. Luckily, Agnes _____ and she told me.

12. I _____ concentrate on my homework with the radio turned on so loudly. _____ you

please ask them to lower the volume?

13. He _____ see anything because it was raining so heavily. Neither _____ he drive properly.

PART 18

請在空格中填入助動詞 can 或 could（若需否定請用縮寫形式）。

1. "_____ you help me with my work?" "Why? _____ you do it by yourself?"

2. He has always been right. He _____ be wrong this time!

3. "_____ you please tell me where the post office is?" he inquired.

4. I _____ work after a late night. I feel too drowsy.

5. "He _____ have meant it, so please don't feel so hurt," she said to me.

6. However hard he tried, he just _____ ride the horse.

7. He had gone home when she arrived, so he _____ have met her that day.

8. "_____ you lend me your ladder for a while, please? I _____ find mine anywhere."

9. Alice asked if she _____ come along with us.

10. "_____ I enter the competition?" the child asked her brother. "No, you _____," he answered. "You're too young."

11. "Look! _____ you see that man? It's Major Carson!" "It _____ be; Major Carson has been posted to Bradsville."

12. "_____ you ask your manager if I _____ speak with him for a moment?" he asked the secretary.

13. "Oh, dear! I _____ remember where I put my glasses," old Mrs. Cook said. "_____ you please help me look for them?"

14. "Don't try to lift that weight. You _____ do it." "Of course, I _____! Just watch this."

15. Peter saw a girl struggling in the deep water, but he _____ help because he himself _____ swim.

16. "I _____ live underground for two weeks!" he boasted. "I bet that you _____ do it even for a single day."

17. I _____ lend you some money if today were payday, but I _____ now.

18. "If you stood on the table, _____ you touch the ceiling?" "I _____ unless I stood on

a chair on the table."

PART 19

請在空格中填入 can、could、can't、couldn't 或 able to。

1. The child asked his mother, "_____ I go to the airport, too?" She replied, "No, you _____."

2. "_____ you please tell me the way to Mr. White's house?" the stranger enquired.

3. She had said that she _____ come, but she didn't turn up yet.

4. He _____ go home after he has finished his work.

5. I _____ see nothing in this thick mist so I have to walk more carefully.

6. "Well, what he has said _____ be true, but I really don't think so," I said.

7. However hard I try, I _____ help worrying about it.

8. Even though the ground was dry and hard, the farmer was _____ plough it.

9. "_____ you lend me your cigarette lighter, please? I _____ find mine anywhere."

10. He _____ jump quite high when he was only nine years old.

11. She was _____ finish her work on time, despite the short notice that she had been given.

12. "_____ you do me a favor?"

13. After she had had the operation, she was _____ walk again.

14. I _____ finish the job today, but I'd rather complete it tomorrow.

15. Listen! _____ you hear the sound of the waves?

16. You _____ do it if you will only put your mind to it.

17. "_____ you take the dog for a walk? I would do it myself if I _____," the old man said to the boy.

18. They _____ have missed the way. I drew a map for them to follow. Even a child of three _____ have found it.

19. He _____ have been there at that time because he was at home.

PART 20

請在空格中填入助動詞 may 或 might。

1. I _____ go to his house if I finish my work quickly.

2. She said that she _____ help me with this problem.

3. _____ I have this painting as well as that one?

4. You _____ tell him whatever you want; I am simply not going to be bothered.

5. He _____ think that it is right, but I know that it is wrong.

6. Do you think that they _____ feel angry if we do not go to their house?

7. I _____ be going to White Sand Beach this Monday if I can get a ride.

8. If they have nothing else to do, they _____ drop in at my house.

9. He wanted to know if he _____ use my brother's bicycle while he was away.

10. You _____ take your book back, but Maria _____ have to wait another day for hers.

11. _____ we borrow a few of your games, please?

12. _____ you have the very best of luck in the coming examination.

13. We thought that they _____ get annoyed if we switched on the radio very loudly.

14. I was told that I _____ have to be fit out with glasses because of my failing eyesight.

PART 21

請在空格中填入助動詞 may 或 might，如句意有必要請改成否定。

1. If I have nothing to do, I _____ visit you.

2. If we run, we _____ just catch the bus.

3. "_____ Lily and I watch you while you paint?" "Yes, you _____."

4. "Our plan _____ work," he said, "or we _____ have to think of another way."

5. "_____ I know your name, please?" the stranger asked.

6. The tale he told _____ or _____ be true.

7. If you had taken the medicine, it _____ have cured your cough.

8. You _____ walk for kilometers among the hills without meeting anyone.

9. Long _____ you live to enjoy your good fortune and _____ you be happy too!

10. She said that she _____ go to the seaside for the holidays.

11. I'll write to her so that she _____ know when to expect us.

PART 22

請在空格中填入助動詞 may 或 might，如句意有必要請改成否定。

1. _____ I borrow your pen for a while?

2. He said that we _____ do what we liked with our spare time.

3. If I go into town, I _____ see him, though it was quite unlikely.

4. You _____ have told me what happened, considering that you're my friend.

5. Since we're here, we _____ as well enjoy ourselves.

6. She _____ want to join the expedition if she knew about it.

7. I _____ climb that mountain if I can find a guide to go with me.

8. _____ you have a pleasant journey!

9. "_____ I use your telephone, please?"

10. Here's my address. I _____ see you again for a long time.

11. The sign reads: "Visitors _____ touch the exhibits."

12. In the desert, you _____ walk a great distance without seeing anyone.

13. Since we've waited for an hour, we _____ as well wait ten minutes more. Who knows, Rodney _____ be on the next bus.

14. He _____ listen to what you say at first, but if you persist he _____ give in.

PART 23

請在空格中填入助動詞 must 或 have to（不能使用 must 的情況），如有需要請改成否定，並注意必要的變化。

1. Do you _____ go now? Can't you stay longer?

2. I have a bad tooth. I _____ see a dentist very soon.

3. We _____ get on the plane at least twenty minutes before it takes off.

4. "You _____ brush your teeth at least twice a day," the dentist told him.

5. In some countries, traffic _____ keep to the left.

6. The signboard says that we _____ not walk on the grass.

7. Maggie _____ stay behind for half an hour yesterday to finish her work.

8. You _____ find a substitute for Kathy; she is ill and cannot take part in the match.

9. All of you _____ see that film. It is really excellent.

10. Your hair is too long. You _____ tie it up or put on a cap.

11. The doctor said, "She is still very ill. I _____ come again tomorrow to see her."

12. Stanley isn't looking too well this morning. Something _____ be wrong with him.

13. We _____ wait for them outside until they came back since we hadn't brought our keys.

14. It's very dark. I _____ light a candle.

15. Since they are in the army, they _____ go wherever they are told to go.

16. We _____ be on our way now. It is already eight o'clock.

17. "You _____ take off those wet clothes at once," his mother told him.

18. I _____ cancel all my outings and games as the examinations were just around the corner.

19. You _____ choose this color. It doesn't suit you at all. You _____ decide on something else.

PART 24

請用 have to 取代 must，將下列句子改寫成現在式和未來式的型態。

1. They must leave this week.

→ _____

→ _____

2. She must go on a diet as she is overweight.

→ _____

→ _____

3. We must not tell them where we are going.

→ _____

→ _____

4. If you fail, you must request a second chance.

→ _____

→ _____

5. The bridge must be repaired by next month.

→ _____

→ _____

6. The ship must sail within the week for Jamaica.

→ _____

→ _____

7. She must clean the windows every week.

→ _____

→ _____

8. The players must practice very hard for the tournament.

→ _____

→ _____

9. You must teach the boys how to put on their ties.

→ _____

→ _____

10. If you see him, tell him that he must bring his documents to the office on Saturday.

→ _____

→ _____

11. The workers must complete the building for the shopping arcade by next year.

→ _____

→ _____

12. He must not sit for the examination this year.

→ _____

→ _____

13. She must see a doctor at once. You must persuade her to go.

→ _____

→ _____

14. The fire must be put out before it spreads to the gas station.

→ _____

→ _____

PART 25

請用 have to 取代 must 來改寫下列句子，並注意必要的變化。

1. He must fill up the car tank with gas before he starts off.

→ _____

2. You must ring him up before he leaves the office.

→ _____

3. She must wait for the five o'clock bus if she misses this one.

→ _____

4. They must read more if they wish to improve their English.

→ _____

5. Must we follow his instructions strictly?

→ _____

6. Jim and Paul must tell her about the mistake.

→ _____

7. His wife must run the shop when he is out.

→ _____

8. Must he always depend on his father for financial support?

→ _____

9. Everyone must obey the rules of the college.

→ _____

10. He must pay all his debts by tomorrow.

→ _____

11. Must I roll up the carpet?

→ _____

12. Every person must go through Customs when entering a foreign country.

→ _____

13. You must wipe the dust from the shelves. Must you always be told what to do?

→ _____

PART 26

請在適當的位置插入 "have to"（注意必要的變化）來改寫下列句子。

1. I will inform her immediately.

→ _____

2. He stayed up late last night to complete his work.

→ _____

3. You practice on your violin regularly for the concert.

→ _____

4. He reported the theft of his new car to the police.

→ _____

5. Aunt Agatha usually goes to the doctor every month to check her blood pressure.

→ _____

基礎文法寶典❹
Essential English Usage & Grammar

6. We will take the dog for treatment tomorrow.

→ _____

7. They stopped at the post office on the way home.

→ _____

8. He wrote out the answers at once.

→ _____

9. You will tell them your address.

→ _____

10. She always pays her rent on the first of the month.

→ _____

11. They will change their clothes before they go out.

→ _____

12. Did she warm the pan first?

→ _____

13. He took his pen with him into the examination hall.

→ _____

14. The workmen will come to repair the roof tomorrow.

→ _____

PART 27

請在空格中填入助動詞 needn't 或 mustn't。

1. I _____ do this; it's not part of my work.

2. He _____ go out today. He isn't well enough yet.

3. You _____ answer in English. You can answer in French if you want.

4. They _____ be allowed to bully the other boys like this.

5. You _____ switch on the flashlight. The intruder might see us.

6. I need your help. You _____ leave me in the lurch.

7. The children _____ leave just yet. They can stay a little longer.

8. You _____ ever do such a foolish thing again. You had everyone worried.

9. We _____ carry the parcels home. The shop will deliver them to our house.

10. He _____ ring the bell. I have the key to the door.

11. We can take care of ourselves, so you _____ worry about us.

12. You _____ worry too much; just concentrate on getting well.

13. They _____ try to persuade me. I've already made up my mind.

14. She _____ take that route. It leads to a dead end.

15. You _____ go to the formal ball in that outfit. You'll be laughed at.

16. We _____ wear a costume if we don't want to.

17. You _____ tell him about the meeting because I've already done so.

18. Tell Mother that she _____ wake me up tomorrow because it is a public holiday.

PART 28

請用 needn't 取代 must 來改寫下列句子，注意句意上的必要變化。

1. I must turn up for practice tomorrow, as I am in the school choir.

    → _____

2. The plaque must be unveiled by the Mayor himself.

    → _____

3. The lawn must be mowed this week.

    → _____

4. She hasn't got much time; she must hurry.

    → _____

5. They have graduated from a commercial school; they must do the accounts.

    → _____

6. The alarm clock must be set to wake us up early tomorrow.

    → _____

7. If the bell rings, you must assemble on the field.

    → _____

8. He must clean and polish his own shoes every day.

    → _____

9. They must send the child back as his parents will not be coming to take him home.

    → _____

10. You must show your passport to the immigration officer.

    → _____

11. She must take both children to the fair.

→ _____

12. They must obtain their parents' permission before going on the excursion.

→ _____

13. We must stay to help them to clear the table.

→ _____

14. Some of the players are absent. We must postpone the match.

→ _____

PART 29

請在空格中填入助動詞 dare、ought to 或 used to，如句意有必要請改成否定。

1. It is very dark. I _____ have brought my flashlight.

2. _____ you dive from the springboard?

3. At one time, people _____ think that the earth was flat.

4. He _____ speak so rudely. It's no wonder that he doesn't have any friends.

5. What happened to the row of houses that _____ be there?

6. "You bully! How _____ you hit that small boy!"

7. You _____ have driven him off into the rain. He'll catch cold.

8. He _____ have a room all to himself when he was young.

9. She _____ tie her hair up in such hot weather.

10. I don't know whether he _____ jump over it. Do you think he _____?

11. That boy _____ bring us fresh milk from the farm every day, but now he doesn't.

12. That shopkeeper _____ be more friendly to his customers if he wants to have more business.

13. "How _____ you say such a thing! You _____ be ashamed of yourself!"

14. Someone _____ stop him from going there. I _____ do that as I do not know him very well.

15. I don't know what is troubling her. She _____ be very cheerful, didn't she?

16. "Billy, you _____ have completed your work by now. You _____ be quite fast. What is wrong with you?" the teacher said.

17. You _____ ask him for more money. He _____ give you quite a lot to spend. You

_____ remind him of that.

18. I _____ say they will never win the championship.

Chapter 14 不定詞

14-0 基本概念

不定詞主要由「to + 原形動詞」構成，如 to go、to find 等。不定詞在句子中可以當作名詞、形容詞或副詞。

14-1 不定詞的用法

(a) 不定詞當名詞時，可以作句子的主詞，須搭配單數動詞。

USAGE PRACTICE

▶ **To drive** like that is foolish. 像那樣開車很愚蠢。

▶ **To believe** such nonsense shows how immature you are.
相信這樣的胡言亂語顯示你是多麼不成熟。

▶ **To err** is human, **to forgive**, divine. 犯錯是人之常情，寬恕是神聖之舉。

▶ **To talk** about doing it is one thing; **to do** it is another. 説是一回事；做又是另一回事。

(b) 不定詞當名詞時，也可以作動詞或動詞片語的受詞。

USAGE PRACTICE

▶ She wanted **to leave** early. 她想要早點離開。

▶ You must learn **to read** well. 你必須學著好好閱讀。

▶ He hopes **to continue** his studies abroad. 他希望出國進修。

▶ She promised **to return** the money. 她答應要還錢。

▶ They remembered **to bring** me the book. 他們記得要把那本書帶來給我。

▶ We agreed **to go** with them. 我們同意和他們一起去。

▶ The guard refused **to let** us in. 警衛拒絕讓我們進入。

▶ He would like **to go** with his parents to Singapore. 他想要和他的父母去新加坡。

▶ She would like **to enter** the swimming competition. 她想要參加游泳比賽。

(c) 不定詞當名詞時，還可以作補語。

▶ To see is **to believe**. 眼見為憑。（主詞補語）

▶ They seem **to be** searching for something. 他們似乎在尋找某物。（主詞補語）

▶ He appears **to take** the matter very lightly. 他對這件事情似乎蠻不在乎。（主詞補語）

▶ They asked us **to help** them. 他們要求我幫助他們。（受詞補語）

(d) 不定詞當形容詞時，可以用來修飾名詞或代名詞。

▶ Do you have anything for me **to correct** now? 你有任何東西要我現在改正的嗎？

▶ Here is a house **to rent**. 這是一間要出租的房子。

▶ That was indeed a foolish thing **to do**. 那的確是一件蠢事。

▶ Do you have something for me **to eat**? 你有東西可以給我吃嗎？

▶ He wore a bright red shirt and a tie **to match**. 他穿一件鮮紅襯衫，配上一條領帶。

▶ Do you have any wax **to polish** the floor with? 你有沒有用來擦亮地板的蠟？

▶ They have a large garden **to play** in. 他們有很大的花園可以在裡面玩。

▶ She has many dresses **to iron**. 她有很多衣服要燙。

▶ There are sheets **to be** mended. 有床單要縫補。

▶ She wants someone **to talk** to. 她想要和人說說話。

(e) 不定詞當副詞時，可以用來修飾動詞，大多表示「目的」。

▶ You should work **to support** yourself. 你應該工作來養活自己。

▶ He drew the window shade **to keep out** the sun. 他拉上百葉窗擋陽光。

▶ She drove into the lane **to park** the car there. 她把車子開進巷子停車。

▶ She hung the clothes out **to dry**. 她把衣服掛在外面晾乾。

▶ The man went into the shed **to get** the tools. 那個人走進小屋拿工具。

▶ He whistled loudly **to attract** her attention. 他大聲吹口哨吸引她的注意。

▶ They came **to ask** for help. 他們來求援。

▶ They went to the hospital **to see** their friend. 他們去醫院看他們的朋友。

> ▶ I am going out **to buy** some fruit. 我要出去買一些水果。

> ▶ One should eat **to live**, not live **to eat**. 人應該為了活而吃，而不是為了吃而活。

(f) 不定詞當副詞時，也可以與 only 連用，表示「令人失望的結果」。

USAGE PRACTICE

> ▶ He hurried to the station, only **to find** that the train had gone off.
>
> 他匆匆趕去車站，卻發現火車已經開走。

> ▶ We managed to enter the house, only **to find** it empty.
>
> 我們設法進到屋子裡，卻發現裡面空無一人。

(g) 不定詞當副詞時，還可以修飾某些表示「喜、怒、哀、樂等情緒」（如 pleased、sorry、disappointed、anxious 等）或「個人品性或特質」（如 willing 、careful、kind 等）的形容詞，也可以修飾一般形容詞（如 right、easy、difficult 等），表示「原因或理由」。

USAGE PRACTICE

> ▶ We were very pleased **to meet** him. 我們很高興見到他。

> ▶ I am pleased **to hear** of your success. 我很高興聽到你成功的消息。

> ▶ They were glad **to see** the criminal brought to justice. 他們很高興看見罪犯被法律制裁。

> ▶ I'm sorry **to inform** you of the delay in our plans. 我很遺憾地通知你，我們的計畫延遲了。

> ▶ They were kind **to relieve** the old man of his heavy burden.
>
> 他們好心地幫助老人減輕他的重擔。

> ▶ They are willing **to help** us. 他們願意幫助我們。

> ▶ You were right **to offer** him your help. 你幫助他是正確的。

(h) 不定詞當副詞時，還可以修飾副詞，表示「結果」。

USAGE PRACTICE

> ▶ She was too tired **to walk** any further. 她太疲倦，無法再走了。

> ▶ He was foolish enough **to believe** her. 他真夠傻，竟然會相信她。

> ▶ He was fortunate enough **to win** first prize. 他有夠幸運才能贏得頭獎。

▶ He was kind enough **to help** me out. 他人真好，幫我渡過難關。

▶ Would you be so kind as **to help** me? 你能行行好幫幫我嗎？

14-2 省略 to 的用法

(a) 在某些特定情況下，不定詞的 to 常可以省略，這種沒有 to 的不定詞稱為「原形不定詞 (bare infinitive)」。

> **USAGE PRACTICE**
>
> ▶ You had better not **go** there alone. 你最好不要一個人去那邊。

(b) 原形不定詞用於感官動詞（如 see、watch、feel、hear、notice 等）之後，即「感官動詞 + 受詞 + 原形不定詞」。

> **USAGE PRACTICE**
>
> ▶ I felt the floor **tremble** under me. 我感覺地板在我腳下震動。
>
> ▶ We watched the train **pull** out of the station. 我們看見火車駛離車站。
>
> ▶ They are watching us **play** chess. 他們正在看我們下棋。
>
> ▶ She watched him **lift** the child to his shoulders. 她看他把孩子舉起來放在肩膀上。
>
> ▶ I heard her **cry** at night. 我聽到她晚上在哭泣。
>
> ▶ He heard her **sing** just now. 他剛才聽到她唱歌。
>
> ▶ We heard them **whisper** in the room. 我們聽到他們在房間裡面低聲講話。
>
> ▶ I saw him **take** the books. 我看見他拿了那些書。
>
> ▶ We saw him **put up** the shelves. 我們看見他安裝那些架子。
>
> ▶ I saw him **pick up** something from the floor. 我看見他從地板上撿起某個東西。

 感官動詞後面該用原形不定詞或現在分詞很容易被混淆。兩者在意思上很接近，但是原形不定詞表示「已完成的持續性動作」，而現在分詞則強調「正在進行」的意思。（分詞用法詳見 **16–1**）

▶ I saw him **cross** the road. 我看見他過馬路。（不定詞：他已經到路的另一邊）

▶ I saw him **crossing** the road. 我看見他正穿越馬路。（現在分詞：他正要走到路的另一邊）

▶ She heard him **come** in. 她聽到他進來。（不定詞：他已經進來了）

▶ She heard him **coming** in. 她聽到他正進門來。（現在分詞：他正要進來）

(c) 原形不定詞用於使役動詞（如 make、have、let 等）之後，即「使役動詞 + 受詞 + 原形不定詞」。

▶ My father made me **go** out of the room. 我爸爸要我離開房間。

▶ The salesman made us **buy** his products. 業務員要我們買他的商品。

▶ They made him **return** the stolen article. 他們要他歸還被偷的物品。

▶ She made him **work** hard. 她要他努力工作。

▶ She had us **clean** up the mess. 她要我們整理這一團混亂。

▶ I will let you **see** the album later. 等一下我會讓你看相簿。

▶ They let us **use** their bicycles. 他們讓我們使用他們的腳踏車。

▶ The carpenter let us **use** his tools. 這木匠讓我們用他的工具。

(d) 原形不定詞也用於以下動詞或片語之後：help、had better、would rather、cannot help but 等。

▶ He helped me **compile** the book. 他幫我編書。

▶ She would rather **take** the bus than **run** all the way. 她寧可搭公車而不願意一路跑步。

▶ He cannot help but **accept** the judge's decision. 他不得不接受法官的決定。

14-3 不定詞的慣用語

(a) due 後面常接不定詞，表示「預定要做的事」。

▶ Hurry up! The plane is due **to leave** now. 快點！班機要起飛了。

▶ The match is due **to start** at five o'clock. 比賽預定在五點開始。

▶ The film is due **to be shown** on Saturday. 這電影預定在週六上映。

(b) be 動詞與不定詞連用時，表示「職責、義務、意圖、約定、可能性」等意思，常譯為「應該做…、必須做…；預定做…；會做…」。

▶ You are **to take** your medicine three times a day. 你一天要服藥三次。

▶ He was **to take** the car to the repair shop. 他要把車開到維修廠。

▶ You are **to report** to the office at once. 你必須立刻到辦公室報到。

▶ How am I **to answer** this letter? 我應該如何回覆這封信？

▶ All students are **to assemble** in the hall. 所有學生都會在禮堂集合。

▶ She is not **to take** it without the owner's permission. 沒有主人的許可，她不應該拿走它。

(c) 一般動詞 have 與不定詞連用時，表示「必須，不得不」。

▶ I have **to study** now. 我現在必須讀書。

▶ She has **to finish** her work soon. 她必須很快地完成她的工作。

▶ Do you have **to submit** your forms by today? 你必須在今天以前繳交你的表格嗎？

▶ Every student had **to recite** a poem. 每個學生必須背誦一首詩。

(d) about 後面接不定詞時，表示「即將要做或要發生的事」。

▶ He is about **to leave** the house. 他即將要離開家。

(e) need 和 dare 當作一般動詞（非助動詞）時，後面必須接不定詞。

▶ Do you think he would dare **to blackmail** her? 你認為他敢敲詐她嗎？

▶ She doesn't need **to buy** so much cloth. 她不需要買這麼多的布料。

(f) 有時可以用 to 來代表整個不定詞，以避免重複先前提過的動詞或片語。

▶ We will go if you want **to**. 如果你想去，我們會去。

▶ He would like to attend your party, but he's afraid that he won't be able **to**.

他想參加你的派對，但是恐怕無法成行。

基礎文法寶典❹
Essential English Usage & Grammar

▶ "I don't know how to do it." "You ought **to**." 「我不知道該怎麼做。」「你應該知道的。」

▶ "Won't you have some more tea?" "Yes, I would love **to**."

「你要不要再喝點茶？」「好的，我想再喝點。」

14-4 不定詞的句型

(a) 疑問詞 (how/what/which/...) + to V...

USAGE PRACTICE

▶ He doesn't know how **to repair** cars. 他不知道如何修理車子。

▶ Do you know what **to bring** to the picnic? 你知道要帶什麼去野餐嗎？

▶ She knows when **to take** her medicine. 她知道什麼時候該吃藥。

▶ Show him where **to put** the instruments. 告訴他要把這些儀器放在哪裡。

(b) it + is/was + 形容詞 + to V...

USAGE PRACTICE

▶ It is hard **to admit** that you are wrong. 要承認自己錯了很難。

▶ It isn't wrong **to say** that they are to blame. 説他們該受譴責並沒有錯。

▶ It was silly **to have** such ideas. 有這樣的想法是愚蠢的。

▶ It is easy **to talk** about solving it but difficult **to find** the solution.

用嘴巴説要解決很容易，但要找到解決方法卻很難。

▶ It is odd **to think** that I might have been selected.

認為我可能已經被選上了是很奇怪的（想法）。

 此句型中，虛主詞 it 代替真正的主詞（即不定詞），而不定詞則往後移。如果在此句型中的形容詞後加上「of/for + 人」時，可以表示「對某人的評論或某事對某人的影響」。

▶ It was kind of him **to give** us a lift. 他真好心，能搭載我們一程。

▶ It was stupid of him **to bring** it up. 他真傻，竟然提起這件事。

▶ It was generous of her **to lend** me the book. 她真慷慨，借我這本書。

▶ It is good for you **to have** such a friend. 你有這樣的朋友真好。

(c) 不定詞也可以用在感嘆句中，或當作獨立不定詞來修飾句子。

不定詞
Chapter 14

▶ "Oh, **to be** a child again!" 「噢，但願能回到童年！」

▶ **To think** that she was here all the time! 想不到她一直在這裡！

▶ **To be** frank with you, I think that you're wrong. 坦白說，我認為你錯了。

14-5 不定詞的時態和語態

(a) 以下是用 do 為例，列出不定詞的各種時態與語態。

		簡單式	進行式	完成式	完成進行式
主	動	to do	to be doing	to have done	to have been doing
被	動	to be done	×	to have been done	×

▶ This house is **to be sold**. 這棟房子將出售。

▶ They are **to be engaged** in December. 他們將在十二月訂婚。

▶ He says that the plane is **to be leaving for New York**. 他說那架飛機將飛往紐約。

▶ **To be blamed** for something that you didn't do is downright unfair!

為了你沒做過的事而被責備是完全不公平的！

▶ I'll show you the rooms **to be tidied**. 我會帶你去看要整理的房間。

▶ After three hours of hard work, nothing else remained **to be done**.

在三小時辛苦的工作後，沒有其他要做的事了。

▶ That box is too heavy **to be carried**. 那個箱子太重，扛不起來。

▶ He is **to be rewarded** for his brave action. 他將因為他的英勇行為而得到獎勵。

▶ The work had **to be finished** as soon as possible. 這個工作必須盡快完成。

▶ He appears **to be bored** by the story. 他似乎對這個故事感到厭煩。

▶ **To have heard** him sing was wonderful. 聽過他唱歌是很棒的事。

▶ It is clever of you **to have found** the solution to our problem.

你真聰明，找到解決我們問題的方法。

▶ We should like **to have been told** about this earlier. 我們會想要早點被告知這件事。

(b) 不定詞的完成式可以用來表示「比主動詞更早發生的動作」。

USAGE PRACTICE

▶ I am sorry **to have said** such a thing. 我很抱歉我說了這樣的話。

▶ She will be sorry **to have missed** you. 沒看到你，她會很遺憾。

▶ They seem **to have disappeared** from the village. 他們好像已經從村子裡消失了。

 不定詞的完成式也可以用來表示「之前該做而沒做的事」。

▶ We were **to have gone** there yesterday. 我們昨天原本要去那裡的。(但我們沒有去)

▶ I was **to have finished** it yesterday, but I didn't do so. 本來我昨天要把它完成的，但我沒有。

Chapter 14　應用練習

PART 1

請依提示在空格中填入正確的不定詞形式。

1. I saw the boy _____ (*steal*) an orange from the stall.

2. Will you please help me _____ (*take*) some of these parcels?

3. I have _____ (*leave*) right now because my mother has told me _____ (*go*) back by six-thirty.

4. They refused to let the little girl _____ (*go*) with them on the picnic.

5. Mr. Jones went to the bank _____ (*withdraw*) some money, but he forgot _____ (*bring*) his savings book with him.

6. He cannot help but _____ (*accept*) the invitation, since they pressed it on him.

7. The tourists watched the natives _____ (*perform*) the Harvest Dance.

8. The teacher told us _____ (*gather*) in the hall because the principal wanted us _____ (*attend*) the prize-giving ceremony.

9. No one helped me _____ (*make*) the cake, but all of them offered to help me _____ (*eat*) it.

10. We'd better _____ (*inform*) them of the change in the time of the meeting.

11. We need a large box _____ (*put*) these books in. Ask Mother _____ (*give*) us one of the boxes in the shed.

12. I'll teach you how _____ (*do*) it one of these days.

13. He felt the earth _____ (*tremble*) beneath his feet and knew that it was an earthquake.

14. He offered _____ (*give*) us a lift and told us that he would drop us off near our school.

15. Would you like _____ (*have*) a drink before you go?

16. Would you rather _____ (*play*) chess, or shall we have a game of cards?

17. You were told not _____ (*do*) that.

18. He stopped on the way _____ (*talk*) with a friend.

19. We had better _____ (*study*) harder this term, since Father has promised us a treat if we pass the examination.

20. I have _____ (*go*) right now because I have something important _____ (*do*).

21. Posters are _____ (*put*) up in conspicuous places in town.

22. It is impossible _____ (*persuade*) him _____ (*lend*) us his scooter.

23. The color will fade if she hangs that dress out in the sun _____ (*dry*).

24. He is too tired _____ (*open*) his eyes.

PART 2

請依提示在空格中填入正確的不定詞形式。

1. "We'd better _____ (*clean*) up the mess before Mother comes back," Eddie said.

2. Did they manage _____ (*bring*) the book that you wanted?

3. All of us were warned not _____ (*go*) to the beach, since a typhoon is approaching.

4. The widow watched her son _____ (*sing*) and _____ (*dance*) among the other children, and she felt tears _____ (*roll*) down her cheeks.

5. We were _____ (*go*) by train to the city.

6. I felt someone _____ (*tap*) me on the shoulder, so I turned around.

7. You had better _____ (*bring*) an umbrella with you; it might start _____ (*rain*) any minute now.

8. Can you please ask them _____ (*keep*) quiet?

9. His father wouldn't let him _____ (*drive*) the car even though he has a driver's license.

10. I saw him _____ (*run*) toward the stranger and _____ (*give*) him a small package wrapped in brown paper.

11. Do you think she would dare _____ (*talk*) back to her boss?

12. They made us _____ (*clean*) the whole house before they let us _____ (*take*) a rest.

13. She did her best, but she failed _____ (*break*) the record.

14. Some newspaper reporters have come _____ (*interview*) the minister.

15. The meeting is due _____ (*start*) at one o'clock.

16. Remember _____ (*bring*) these books to Cecilia when you go to her house tomorrow.

17. I don't think it is necessary _____ (*bring*) along all your books.

18. No one is allowed _____ (*enter*) without a ticket.

19. What kind of tool should we use _____ (*repair*) the fence?

20. The fish has _____ (*clean*) properly before you cook it.

21. Please remind me _____ (*turn*) off the lights before I leave the house.

22. My sister wants _____ (*be*) a doctor when she grows up.

23. _____ (*be*) honest would be a good policy.

24. Would you be so good as _____ (*give*) me a hand?

PART 3

請用不定詞取代粗體部分，改寫下列句子。

1. That story sounds **as though it were** true.

   → _____

2. I was told **that I must not leave** the room.

   → _____

3. Have you got anything for us **that we can eat**?

   → _____

4. She hopes **that she will be chosen** to represent her school.

   → _____

5. We must wait **till we hear** the results of the contest.

   → _____

6. You will have to study hard **so that you will pass** the examination.

   → _____

7. The first person **who reaches** the finish line will be declared the winner.

   → _____

8. Is there anything else **that we should discuss**?

→ _____

9. The girl did not expect **that she would get** the job.

→ _____

10. The poacher was warned **that he should not trespass** on the estate again.

→ _____

11. The doctor advised Mr. Biggs **that he should not smoke**.

→ _____

12. Will you promise **that you will not lose** this magazine?

→ _____

13. I hope **that I'll receive** the letter by tomorrow.

→ _____

14. We understood what needed **doing** when the time came.

→ _____

15. I expect **that I will complete** writing the book by next Christmas.

→ _____

16. The last person **who finished** had to stay behind to clean up the mess.

→ _____

17. Amy was told **that she should not go out** alone in the dark.

→ _____

18. She had to wait a long time **before buying** the tickets.

→ _____

19. The boy scouts hope **that they will reach** the summit by nightfall.

→ _____

20. It appears **that it is** an impossible task.

→ _____

Chapter 15 動名詞

15-0 基本概念

動名詞由動詞字尾加上 ing 形成，具有名詞的性質，在句子中可以當作主詞和受詞。

15-1 動名詞的用法

(a) 動名詞可以置於句首，當作句子的主詞，必須搭配單數動詞。

USAGE PRACTICE

▶ **Smoking** is bad for health. 吸煙有害健康。

▶ **Smoking** is forbidden here. 此處禁止吸煙。

▶ **Singing** folk songs is enjoyable. 唱民歌很令人愉快。

▶ **Reading** occupies a lot of his time. 閱讀佔用他很多時間。

▶ **Fishing** requires a lot of patience. 釣魚需要很大的耐心。

▶ **Climbing** mountains is a sport, too. 爬山也是一項運動。

▶ **Swimming** tones up body muscles. 游泳強化身體的肌肉。

▶ **Painting** a portrait requires a lot of concentration. 畫一幅肖像需要全神貫注。

▶ **Watching** a football game is quite exciting. 觀賞美式足球賽非常刺激。

▶ **Working** in these conditions is intolerable. 在這些狀況下工作令人無法忍受。

▶ **Sleeping** in the afternoon gives me a headache. 睡午覺令我頭痛。

▶ **Fighting** with that boy was a most foolish thing to do. 跟那個男孩打架是非常愚蠢的事。

▶ **Breaking** his promise was his greatest mistake. 不遵守諾言是他最大的錯誤。

▶ **Redecorating** the house was a tough job. 重新裝潢這房子是件棘手的工作。

▶ **Sitting** up late at night to watch television is not good for children.
熬夜看電視對孩子們是不好的。

(b) 動名詞常置於下列的動詞（或動詞片語）之後，當作受詞。

USAGE PRACTICE

begin 開始	need 需要	deny 否認	detest 厭惡
try 嘗試	bear 忍受	allow 允許	escape 逃避

---

remember 記得	postpone 延遲	risk 冒…的危險	enjoy 喜愛
avoid 避免	imagine 想像	mind 介意	miss 錯過
hate 不喜歡	finish 完成	practice 練習	excuse 辯解
stop 停止	like 喜歡	dislike 厭惡	love 愛好
consider 考慮	continue 繼續	cease 停止	mention 提到
forbid 禁止	resent 怨恨	suggest 提議	delay 推遲
admit 承認	keep 繼續		

▶ Do you like **watching** television？ 你喜歡看電視嗎？

▶ I enjoyed **eating** those crabs. 我喜歡吃那些螃蟹。

▶ She enjoys **listening** to the stories her mother tells her. 她喜歡聽媽媽講的故事。

▶ He has just finished **changing** the tire. 他才剛換好輪胎。

▶ The floor needs **washing**; it is covered with dirt. 地板滿是灰塵，需要清洗。

▶ I don't think the house needs **repainting**. 我不認為這房子需要重新油漆。

▶ I remember **seeing** him in Michael's house. 我記得在邁可家看過他。

▶ She hates **doing** housework. 她厭惡做家事。

▶ He suggested **setting** up a fair to raise funds. 他提議辦一個義賣會來籌募資金。

▶ Will you stop **fooling** around? 你不要再遊手好閒了好嗎？

▶ We tried to avoid **meeting** him. 我們試著避免遇見他。

▶ She denied **bribing** the man. 她否認賄賂了那個人。

▶ They began **talking** about something else when she entered.
當她進來時，他們開始談論其他事。

▶ They resented **working** under him. 他們討厭在他的手下工作。

▶ You can't keep on **eating** bread every day. 你不能每天一直吃麵包。

▶ She kept on **insisting** that she needed no help at all. 她一直堅稱她一點都不需要協助。

▶ I gave up **trying** to convince her. 我放棄試著去說服她。

▶ They burst out **laughing** at his joke. 聽了他的笑話，他們大笑起來。

 注意 mind 當動詞時表示「介意」，後面常接動名詞，尤其用於否定句和疑問句中。

▶ Do you mind **waiting** a few minutes more? 你介意再等幾分鐘嗎？
▶ Would you mind **hanging** this painting up for me? 你介意幫我把這幅畫掛上嗎？

▶ They did not mind **traveling** in the old car. 他們不介意搭舊車旅行。

▶ Do you mind **going** out for a second? 你介意離開一下嗎？

▶ Would you mind **speaking** more clearly? 能不能請你說得更清楚一點呢？

▶ I wouldn't mind **telling** you the truth. 我不介意告訴你事實。

▶ You mustn't mind **working** hard if you wish to stay on. 如果你希望留任，就不可以介意辛苦工作。

(c) 動名詞也可以置於介系詞後面，當作受詞；而這些介系詞常放在動詞或形容詞的後面。

USAGE PRACTICE

▶ He is very keen on **rearing** chickens. 他很熱衷養雞。

▶ I'm sick of **eating** the same food every day. 我厭倦每天吃同樣的食物。

▶ She is sick of **lying** in bed every day. 她對每天臥床感到厭倦。

▶ They don't know much about **developing** photographs. 他們對沖洗照片不甚了解。

▶ He is capable of **looking** after the house. 他能照料這間房子。

▶ I am used to **doing** all the work by myself. 我習慣獨自做所有的工作。

▶ She is fond of **sitting** in a corner and **daydreaming**. 她喜歡坐在角落，做白日夢。

▶ He was accused of **telling** lies. 他被指控說謊。

▶ Most people find relaxation in **swimming**. 大部分的人發現游泳可以讓人放鬆。

▶ Aren't you afraid of **getting** sick just before the examination? 你不怕在考試前生病嗎？

▶ Those boys are intent on **winning** the game. 那些男孩一心一意想要贏得比賽。

▶ She is good at **teaching** mentally challenged children. 她擅長教導智能不足的兒童。

▶ Pauline is not good at **cooking** or **washing**. 寶琳不擅長烹飪或洗滌。

▶ My brother is good at **repairing** clocks and watches. 我的兄弟擅長於修理鐘錶。

▶ They are accustomed to **waking** up early every morning.

他們習慣每天早晨都很早起床。

▶ He persisted in **breaking** the school rules. 他一直破壞校規。

▶ She is really worried about **passing** the examination. 她十分擔心能否通過考試。

15-2 動名詞與不定詞的比較

(a) 動名詞常用來代替不定詞。

USAGE PRACTICE	
不定詞	動名詞
▶ She likes **to dance**. 她喜歡跳舞。	▶ She likes **dancing**. 她喜歡跳舞。

(b) 當指特定狀況時，多使用不定詞；而動名詞多指一般情形。

USAGE PRACTICE	
不定詞	動名詞
▶ I like **to watch** television tonight. 我今晚想看電視。(特定狀況：今晚)	▶ I like **watching television**. 我喜歡看電視。(一般情形)
▶ She hates **to read** when there are people around. 她不喜歡在週遭有人時讀書。(特定狀況：週遭有人時)	▶ She hates **reading**. 她不喜歡讀書。(一般情形)
▶ "Do you like **to see** a film tonight?" "No, I prefer **to stay** at home." 「你今晚想看電影嗎？」「不，我寧願留在家裡。」(特定狀況：今晚的兩個活動)	▶ I prefer **staying** at home to **seeing** a film at the movie theater. 我寧願待在家裡而不願去電影院看電影。(一般的兩個活動)
▶ It's raining. I'd advise you **to take** a bus rather than **to walk**. 下雨了。我建議你搭公車而不要走路。(特定狀況：下雨)	▶ **Walking** is more pleasant than **taking a bus**. 走路比搭公車還令人愉快。(一般的兩個活動)

15-3 動名詞語意上的主詞

(a) 當動名詞語意上的主詞與主句的主詞不同時，須以「所有格 + 動名詞」表示動名詞語意上的主詞。

USAGE PRACTICE
▶ Do you mind my **using** your computer? 你介意我使用你的電腦嗎？
▶ I don't like Helen's **coming** late at all. 我一點也不喜歡海倫遲到。
▶ He doesn't like Lucy's **going** home alone in the dark. 他不喜歡露西在黑暗中單獨回家。
▶ Please excuse our **making** so much noise. 請原諒我們製造了這麼多噪音。

▶ I don't remember his **giving** us any instructions. 我不記得他有給我們任何指示。

▶ I remembered their **talking** about the accident. 我記得他們談論到這場意外。

▶ He objected to Timmy's **joining** us on the trip. 他反對提米和我們一起旅行。

▶ They were disturbed by the cat's **meowing**. 他們被貓的叫聲打擾到了。

▶ We dislike his **interfering** with our work. 我們討厭他干涉我們的工作。

▶ They weren't pleased at your **asking** them for more money.

他們不高興你向他們要求更多的錢。

 但是，在口語中，受格可以取代所有格，指涉動名詞語意上的主詞。

▶ You wouldn't mind me **using** it, would you? 你不會介意我用它，對吧？

▶ They resented him **saying** such things about them. 他們很生氣他說了有關他們的這些事情。

▶ We are accustomed to Mary **complaining** about the weather all the time.

我們習慣了瑪莉老是抱怨天氣。

▶ He doesn't like Lucy **going** home alone in the dark. 他不喜歡露西在黑暗中單獨回家。

▶ Please excuse us **making** so much noise. 請原諒我們製造了這麼多噪音。

▶ I don't remember him **giving** us any instructions. 我不記得他有給我們任何指示。

▶ I remembered them **talking** about the accident. 我記得他們談論到這場意外。

▶ He objected to Timmy **joining** us on the trip. 他反對提米和我們一起旅行。

▶ She was annoyed at you **interrupting** her speech. 她對你打斷她的演講感到生氣。

(b) 當動名詞語意上的主詞是無生物時，不用所有格，改用主格，指涉動名詞語意上的主詞。

USAGE PRACTICE

▶ There's no sign of the bus **coming**. 沒有公車要來的跡象。

▶ There's no sign of the dinner **appearing**. 沒有晚餐要上桌的跡象。

15-4 動名詞的慣用語

(a) come/go + V-ing

USAGE PRACTICE

▶ Will you come **hiking** with us during the holidays? 你假日期間要和我們一起去健行嗎？

▶ Won't you come **shopping/sightseeing** with me? 你不和我一起去購物／觀光嗎？

▶ The men have planned to go **hunting** this weekend. 這些人已經計畫好這週末要去打獵。

▶ He wants to go **swimming** next week. 他下週想去游泳。

(b) be + busy/worth/worthwhile + V-ing

USAGE PRACTICE

▶ My mother is busy **cooking** dinner. 我媽媽正忙著煮晚飯。

▶ The manager was busy **signing** some letters. 經理正忙著簽署一些信件。

▶ He is too busy **trimming** the hedge to have his tea. 他正忙著修剪樹籬以至於沒時間喝茶。

▶ Most of them are busy **sorting** out their belongings.

他們大部份的人都忙著整理自己的東西。

▶ Is that book worth **buying**? 那本書值得買嗎？

▶ That film is not worth **seeing** at all. 那部影片一點也不值得看。

▶ Such a trivial thing is not worth **worrying** about. 像這樣無足輕重的小事是不值得擔心的。

▶ Is it worthwhile **decorating** the whole house just for this small party?

值得為這小聚會裝飾整個房子嗎？

(c) can't + help/stop + V-ing

USAGE PRACTICE

▶ He couldn't help **telling** the truth. 他不得不說實話。

▶ I can't help **wondering** what will happen to the orphans.

我忍不住想知道那些孤兒會發生什麼事。

▶ We can't help **talking** during the break. 我們忍不住在休息時間說話。

▶ I couldn't help **overhearing** their remarks about me. 我忍不住偷聽他們對我的批評。

▶ We couldn't help **bursting** into laughter when we saw the monkeys dancing together.

當看到這些猴子一起跳舞時，我們忍不住大笑。

▶ His mother can't stop **worrying** about his health. 他的母親一直擔心他的健康。

(d) it is no use/good (+ 所有格) + V-ing...

▶ It's no use **advising** him against it. He's too stubborn.

建議他不要做這件事是沒用的。他太頑固了。

▶ It's no use **crying** over spilled milk. 覆水難收。

▶ It's no use **persuading** him. Once he has made up his mind, he won't change it.

勸他是沒有用的，他一旦下定決心就不會改變。

▶ It's no use your **telling** me you're sorry. 你對我說抱歉也無濟於事。

▶ It is no use my **approaching** them for help. 我向他們求援是沒有用的。

▶ It's no good **crying** over what you've done. It won't help you at all.

為你已經做的事哭泣沒什麼好處，那對你一點幫助也沒有。

▶ It's no good **following** the instructions that she gave you. 照她給你的指示去做也是沒用。

(e) it is a waste of time + V-ing...

▶ It's a waste of time **asking** him to help. 要求他幫忙是浪費時間。

15-5 動名詞的時態和語態

(a) 以下是用 do 為例，列出動名詞的各種時態與語態。因為動名詞與現在分詞型態相同，而現在分詞本身就是構成進行式的要素，所以動名詞並沒有另外的進行式形態。

	簡單式	完成式
主　動	doing	having done
被　動	being done	having been done

(b) 動名詞的被動形式是由 "being + 過去分詞" 所構成。

▶ He escaped **being caught** in the nick of time. 他及時逃跑沒被捉住。

▶ Johnny dislikes **being pinched** on the arm. 強尼不喜歡被人捏手臂。

▶ She is hopeful of **being chosen** for the job. 她希望能被選上來做這份工作。

▶ I had nothing to do with your **being told** to stay after school.

　你被要求放學後留下來這件事情與我無關。

▶ **Being defeated** is unpleasant. 被人打敗是令人不愉快的。

▶ **Being tricked** by the small boy hurt her pride. 被這個小男孩欺騙傷害了她的自尊心。

▶ **Being** stared at like that is not pleasant at all! 像那樣子被注視一點也不令人愉快!

▶ He dislikes **being told** what to do. 他不喜歡被吩咐要做什麼。

(c) 動名詞的完成式表示比主句動詞更早發生的動作或狀態。

▶ He regretted **having told** us the secret. 他後悔把祕密告訴我們。

▶ He complained about **having been ordered** to vacate his room.

　他抱怨被命令空出他的房間。

▶ **Having been expelled** is nothing to boast about! 已經被開除不是什麼好自誇的事!

小練習

請根據提示在空格中填入正確的動名詞形式。

1. _____ (*swim*) is a good form of exercise.

2. _____ (*walk*) alone in the dark can be quite dangerous.

3. His hobbies are _____ (*sing*) and _____ (*dance*).

4. My brother was very keen on _____ (*play*) basketball when he was young.

5. The twins are very fond of _____ (*fish*).

6. Those recruits need _____ (*train*) before they can be sent to work in the factory.

7. _____ (*look*) for a suitable house in the city is quite a difficult job.

8. _____ (*walk*) to the bus stop from here will take some time.

9. _____ (*paint*) with watercolors can be fun.

10. Paul is not much good at _____ (*take*) care of children.

11. When he had finished _____ (*read*) the book, he went home.

12. She thinks it is not worth _____ (*pay*) a visit to the museum.

13. _____ (*lie*) on the beach is quite relaxing.

14. Martin is busy _____ (*wash*) his car in the garage.

15. Those two men are experts at _____ (*tumble*), for they used to be in the circus.

16. _____ (*drill*) a hole through the cement floor is quite a difficult task.

17. Does he like _____ (*smoke*) cigars?

18. We prefer _____ (*play*) the piano to _____ (*play*) the violin.

☞ 更多相關習題請見本章應用練習 Part 1～Part 5。

Chapter 15　應用練習

PART 1

請根據提示在空格中填入正確的動名詞形式。

1. She can come _____ (*shop*) with us if she wants to.

2. _____ (*work*) as a teacher is not always unpleasant.

3. He is busy _____ (*fix*) his bicycle in the garage.

4. After so many weeks of neglect, the lawn requires _____ (*mow*).

5. Terry and Robin are fond of _____ (*play*) jokes on other people.

6. These boys enjoy _____ (*bully*) the smaller boys as much as they enjoy _____ (*throw*) stones at dogs and cats.

7. Do you want to go _____ (*swim*) with us?

8. _____ (*collect*) stamps is one of my hobbies; _____ (*garden*) is another one.

9. _____ (*smoke*) is not allowed in a gas station since gasoline is highly inflammable.

10. The robber entered the house by _____ (*break*) the lock.

11. They are quite used to _____ (*get*) up early in the morning.

12. His mother worried about his _____ (*spend*) too much time _____ (*surf*) the Internet.

13. All of them are interested in _____ (*watch*) soccer games.

14. The naughty boy has been punished for _____ (*break*) the vase.

15. Did the policeman fine you for _____ (*speed*)?

16. I don't really know much about Andy's _____ (*quit*) his job.

17. Do you think that these shirts are worth _____ (*buy*)?

18. I don't mind their _____ (*share*) my food.

PART 2

請根據提示在空格中填入正確的動名詞形式，部分還需加上所有格。

1. I can understand _____ (*you/want*) to go, but are you capable of _____ (*look*) after yourself?

2. A student taking an examination should rely on _____ (*study*) and not on _____ (*guess*).

3. Do you mind _____ (*he/smoke*) a pipe? He can't get used to _____ (*do*) without a smoke after dinner.

4. His mother dislikes _____ (*he/nod*) and _____ (*yawn*) at breakfast time.

5. I hope that your uncle agrees to _____ (*you/come*) to visit me. _____ (*see*) you in person is better than _____ (*write*) to you.

6. She is afraid of _____ (*Philip/lose*) his way in the dark, and I heard _____ (*she/tell*) him to bring a flashlight along.

7. The boy succeeded in _____ (*swim*) the full length of the pool. Now, he intends to make himself good at_____ (*dive*).

8. Mother hates _____ (*us/eat*) and_____ (*drink*) between meals, but we can't help _____ (*do*) so as we have been doing it ever since we were little.

9. I remember _____ (*she/borrow*) a book from me, but I don't remember _____ (*she/return*) it at all.

10. My father doesn't like the idea of _____ (*I/learn*) to ride a motorcycle although I keep _____ (*tell*) him that I won't hurt myself.

11. I don't recollect _____ (*you/say*) that you wanted to come. _____ (*make*) room for you now is going to be a problem.

12. _____ (*teach*) that class is a very hard task. Every teacher complains of _____ (*the students/make*) far too much noise.

13. She couldn't resist _____ (*buy*) those red apples.

14. There's no point in _____ (*urge*) the lazy boy to run the errand for you. _____ (*Sleep*) the whole day is all that he ever thinks of.

15. They objected to _____ (*we/leave*) so soon, but we can't risk _____ (*leave*) late as we have to catch the last bus home.

16. The blind are often skillful at _____ (*do*) things with their hands.

17. It's no use _____ (*hurry*) to finish your work and _____ (*make*) a mess of it in the end.

18. They are intent on _____ (*get*) as much money as they can for their club. _____ (*wash*) cars, _____ (*weed*) gardens, and _____ (*do*) chores are all part of their campaign.

PART 3

請根據提示在空格中填入正確的動名詞形式。

1. _____ (*work*) as a salesman gives him a chance to travel. He likes _____ (*travel*) a lot.

2. I wouldn't recommend your _____ (*spend*) money at those gambling dens.

3. Her hobbies are _____ (*swim*) and _____ (*jog*), both of which she is particularly good at.

4. The detective deduced the facts by _____ (*question*) the maid thoroughly. She didn't mind _____ (*tell*) him everything.

5. The clock has always been correct in _____ (*tell*) time.

6. Most of the machines need _____ (*clean*). Imagine _____ (*use*) them for so many months without _____ (*clean*) them.

7. The easiest way of _____ (*learn*) a language is by _____ (*speak*) it and _____ (*read*) books on it.

8. She is dedicated to the task of _____ (*care*) for the sick and _____ (*look*) after the poor.

9. There's no point in _____ (*bear*) things in your heart. The best way of _____ (*get*) rid of a misunderstanding is by _____ (*speak*) it out.

10. When you're free, would you mind _____ (*do*) something for me? The books on the shelf need _____ (*rearrange*) and the silver cups need _____ (*wipe*).

11. My brother is interested in _____ (*collect*) school badges. His collection is really worth _____ (*look*) at!

12. Nothing will be gained by _____ (*go*) against the law.

13. It's a waste of time _____ (*work*) on with this project.

14. We couldn't stop that dog from _____ (*follow*) us wherever we went.

15. I can't bear _____ (*wait*) so long for the bus.

16. Nothing would please me more than _____ (*learn*) that the thief was caught by the police.

17. She couldn't help _____ (*interrupt*) the conversation as they were talking very loudly.

18. Won't you stop _____ (*knock*) on the table? All the noise is giving me a headache.

PART 4

請根據提示在空格中填入正確的動名詞形式，部分還需加上所有格。

1. I can't understand _____ (*he/trick*) by a child.

2. They objected to _____ (*we/talk*) about the incident.

3. She is anxious about _____ (*her brother/come*) late for the appointment.

4. We didn't mind _____ (*they/look*) through our work.

5. It really wasn't worth _____ (*we/stay*) up so late to finish the work.

6. You can't insist on _____ (*he/let*) you off early when there's so much work to be done.

7. I know that your shirt needs _____ (*alter*), but you can't keep _____ (*pester*) me to do it now when I'm so busy.

8. _____ (*you/be*) right this time doesn't mean you are right all the time.

9. Can't you recall _____ (*he/come*) here last time?

10. I was afraid of _____ (*they/leave*) on the tour without me.

11. That blind man is skilled at _____ (*weave*) baskets. I really admire _____ (*he/work*) at such a fast rate.

12. She resents _____ (*I/criticize*) her work so often. She says I always provoke her into _____ (*lose*) her temper.

13. I remember _____ (*I/give*) you explicit instructions, but I don't remember _____ (*you/carry*) out all those instructions.

14. "Excuse _____ (*I/interrupt*) you, girls. Would you please stop _____ (*write*) for a moment?" the teacher asked.

15. Our parents have agreed to _____ (*we/camp*) out in the open, but they are still worried about _____ (*we/get*) proper food.

16. I'm afraid of _____ (*the man/ask*) me questions that I cannot answer.

17. "Would you mind _____ (*I/change*) my seat in the class?" I asked the teacher.

"I'm tired of _____ (*sit*) in the same place all the time."

PART 5

請根據提示在空格中填入正確的動名詞形式。

1. Have you heard of the saying "_____ (*see*) is _____ (*believe*)"?

2. He was already late and couldn't risk _____ (*miss*) the bus.

3. I don't like _____ (*interfere*) in other people's affairs.

4. "Neil, thank you for _____ (*help*) my little brother," she said.

5. The new clerk resented _____ (*tell*) what to do.

6. My youngest brother dislikes _____ (*bathe*) in cold water.

7. _____ (*learn*) English is much easier than _____ (*learn*) French.

8. Mrs. Clark postponed _____ (*make*) a decision until the last minute.

9. She has completed _____ (*pack*) her bags.

10. The chairman left the conference room without _____ (*say*) anything or _____ (*look*) at anyone.

11. Nancy omitted _____ (*put*) a hyphen in the word.

12. Can't you remember _____ (*tell*) me that story just last night?

13. She prefers _____ (*walk*) in the rain to _____ (*take*) a bus.

14. The secretary proposed _____ (*word*) the letter in a more tactful way.

15. _____ (*argue*) with him serves no purpose.

16. The manager does not permit _____ (*smoke*) in the office.

17. The tailor has finished _____ (*sew*) my trousers. Would you mind _____ (*collect*) them for me on your way back?

18. _____ (*chase*) by a fierce dog is not my idea of an exciting adventure!

19. Kevin escaped _____ (*punish*) by _____ (*tell*) his father the truth immediately.

20. We can't risk _____ (*cross*) the desert without first _____ (*make*) preparations for the trip.

PART 6

請根據提示在空格中填入正確的動名詞或不定詞（某些會省略 to）形式。

1. He enjoys _____ (*read*) detective novels.

2. Somebody seems _____ (*turn*) off all the lights; that is why it is so dark.

3. She remembered _____ (*receive*) the parcel from the mailman, and now it is on the table.

4. _____ (*take*) these pills daily will make you strong.

5. I heard him _____ (*say*) that he would come back as soon as he could.

6. We are very anxious _____ (*learn*) that Larry is missing.

7. He didn't mind _____ (*lend*) me his valuable camera.

8. He made me _____ (*wash*) the dirty bicycle and told me not _____ (*use*) it. He just wouldn't let me _____ (*use*) his bicycle.

9. After the storm, the roof needs _____ (*repair*).

10. Did you watch him _____ (*climb*) up that tall tree?

11. Has he finished _____ (*put*) the stamps into his album?

12. She felt her heart _____ (*beat*) faster when she heard strange noises outside.

13. Did your friends manage _____ (*get*) their parents' approval?

14. They have stopped _____ (*write*) us ever since the incident. We haven't heard from them for a long time.

15. I walked over to her house _____ (*say*) hello.

16. Most of us learned _____ (*write*) when we were very young.

17. The workmen are busy _____ (*build*) the house.

18. It was kind of them _____ (*give*) shelter to the orphan.

19. She dislikes _____ (*play*) badminton in the evening.

20. It is quite difficult _____ (*cross*) that flooded river, so you had better _____ (*try*) another route.

PART 7

請根據提示在空格中填入正確的動名詞或不定詞（某些會省略 to）形式。

1. My dog is very good at _____ (*catch*) balls.

2. I saw Peter _____ (*pick*) something up from the floor and _____ (*give*) it to one of his friends.

3. The librarian made me _____ (*return*) the books the next day.

4. My brother has started _____ (*work*) on his report.

5. Nobody heard me _____ (*cry*) for help.

6. You can be fined for _____ (*smoke*) in this national park.

7. We rushed to the movie theater only _____ (*find*) that all the tickets had been sold.

8. The message says that you are _____ (*report*) to your superiors immediately.

9. He has given up _____ (*drink*).

10. The inhabitants of the island were very pleased _____ (*receive*) such souvenirs from the tourists.

11. The lost boy was fortunate enough _____ (*find*) a freshwater stream.

12. My brother is experienced at _____ (*repair*) cars.

13. Will you please tell me when _____ (*give*) the alarm?

14. It's no use _____ (*complain*) about it.

15. The boys were so kind as _____ (*share*) their food with us.

16. The man was accused of _____ (*steal*) the money.

17. My mother doesn't know how _____ (*make*) this kind of chocolate cake.

18. He heard someone _____ (*walk*) toward the door and ran _____ (*lock*) it.

PART 8

請根據提示在空格中填入正確的動名詞或不定詞（某些會省略 to）形式。

1. Please excuse our _____ (*eat*) in the room.

2. _____ (*smoke*) causes ill health. I'd advise you _____ (*give*) up the habit.

3. The students who are taking the examination have been told _____ (*stop*) _____ (*write*).

4. Don't forget _____ (*get*) the magazine back from him. I remember _____ (*lend*) it to him a few weeks ago.

5. It is easier _____ (*say*) something than _____ (*do*) it; _____ (*say*) it is one thing, but _____ (*do*) it is entirely different.

6. _____ (*rise*) early gives me sufficient time _____ (*take*) a walk and also _____ (*have*) breakfast.

7. If you want _____ (*learn*) how _____ (*swim*), you mustn't be afraid of the water.

8. It's no use _____ (*argue*) with him. He will only refuse _____ (*help*) us.

9. Remember _____ (*write*) down all that you have seen on this trip.

10. They have made up their minds not _____ (*play*) against that team.

11. She couldn't bear _____ (*part*) from her family. She insisted on _____ (*come*) home every week.

12. _____ (*have*) an aquarium at home has enabled the children _____ (*learn*) many things about fish.

13. It's a waste of breath _____ (*talk*) to her. She will not agree _____ (*help*) us with this project.

14. _____ (*memorize*) each lesson is not a good way _____ (*study*).

15. He did not forget _____ (*sign*) the documents before he mailed them.

16. As the girls were afraid of _____ (*explore*) the big dark cave, the boys decided not _____ (*explore*) it.

17. Have you finished _____ (*eat*) your lunch? I have something here for you _____ (*repair*).

18. Will you be free _____ (*teach*) me how _____ (*play*) tennis?

PART 9

請根據提示在空格中填入正確的動名詞或不定詞（某些會省略 to）形式。

1. She paid the man some money for _____ (*translate*) the letter.

2. The teacher made Robert _____ (*stay*) behind _____ (*finish*) his work.

3. I don't know how she managed _____ (*finish*) _____ (*make*) all these sandwiches in time.

4. _____ (*go*) to sleep early enables me _____ (*get*) up early, too.

5. I don't remember _____ (*hear*) you say that you had _____ (*go*), too.

6. The doctor advised her _____ (*stop*) _____ (*smoke*), but she didn't bother _____ (*take*) his advice.

7. I enjoy _____ (*rest*) in the afternoon, but these days I don't seem _____ (*have*) the time _____ (*rest*).

8. We went backstage _____ (*watch*) the actors. _____ (*watch*) them from behind the scenes is more interesting than _____ (*watch*) from the hall.

9. If you want _____ (*learn*) how _____ (*parachute*), you must be brave enough _____ (*take*) the risks.

10. "I want you _____ (*rehearse*) the play now," she said. "I won't mind _____ (*stay*)

behind _____ (*direct*) you.”

11. Would you dare _____ (*ask*) him for permission _____ (*use*) his badminton court?

12. She was not able _____ (*enter*) the swimming competition although she tried her best.

13. It is certain _____ (*rain*) later; we'd better _____ (*take*) our umbrellas with us.

14. _____ (*say*) that you are thinking of _____ (*retire*) is ridiculous!

15. She was hurt _____ (*learn*) that they had gone off without _____ (*say*) goodbye to her.

16. _____ (*tell*) the truth, I broke the glass.

17. It was wrong of them _____ (*accuse*) him of _____ (*murder*) the old woman.

18. He made me _____ (*tell*) him the whole story although I didn't want _____ (*do*) so.

PART 10

請根據提示在空格中填入正確的動名詞或不定詞（某些會省略 to）形式。

1. I can't help _____ (*wonder*) whether we should risk _____ (*climb*) that steep rocky path.

2. After a long struggle, the old man gave up _____ (*smoke*) and now prefers _____ (*eat*) chocolate.

3. Keep on _____ (*try*) even if great odds are against you.

4. Please excuse us for _____ (*disturb*) you, but we can't help _____ (*admire*) your paintings.

5. _____ (*sting*) by a jellyfish is not a pleasant sensation at all.

6. That book is worth _____ (*buy*) and _____ (*read*).

7. The boys went _____ (*camp*) at Golden Sands and said that they enjoyed _____ (*swim*) in the sea.

8. He postponed _____ (*leave*) for Hong Kong until the next day.

9. They will be delighted _____ (*know*) that you are in town.

10. Explain to her how she is _____ (*do*) her work.

11. Do you approve of our _____ (*put*) the notice here?

12. It is good of you _____ (*lend*) me your books.

13. She considered _____ (*shift*) next month, but has found nowhere suitable.

14. It is useless _____ (*argue*) with such a stubborn man.

15. You can't risk _____ (*go*) into that burning house. You will get badly burned.

16. There are many things _____ (*do*) before we can leave.

17. He wants you _____ (*tell*) him how _____ (*solve*) that mathematical problem.

Chapter 16 分　詞

16-0 基本概念

分詞是由動詞變化而來，可分為現在分詞 (-ing) 與過去分詞 (-ed)，在句子中可以作為動詞的一部分、形容詞或補語等。

16-1 分詞的種類與用法

(a) 現在分詞可以與 be 動詞形成進行式；過去分詞可以與助動詞 have 形成完成式，或是與 be 動詞形成被動語態。

USAGE PRACTICE

▶ She **is studying** now.　她現在正在讀書。(現在進行式)

▶ They **were playing** in the garden.　他們當時正在花園裡玩。(過去進行式)

▶ He **was working** late in the office.　他當時在辦公室工作到很晚。(過去進行式)

▶ I **have written** the letter.　我已經寫信了。(現在完成式)

▶ He **has arrived** and **has reported** to the officer already.

　他已經到達並向長官報到。(現在完成式)

▶ She **had broken** the vase, but **had not replaced** it with another one.

　她打破了花瓶，但一直沒換上另一個花瓶。(過去完成式)

▶ He **had worked** hard for the examination.　他一直為那個考試而努力唸書。(過去完成式)

▶ The man's life **is dedicated** to helping the sick.

　那個男人的一生奉獻在幫助病人。(被動語態)

(b) 現在分詞和過去分詞都可以當作形容詞，修飾名詞。現在分詞當形容詞時具有主動、進行的涵義；過去分詞當形容詞時則有被動、完成的涵義。

USAGE PRACTICE

現在分詞

an **exciting** story　刺激的故事	a **dancing** girl　跳舞的女孩
a **working** man　正在工作的人	a **sleeping** baby　正在睡覺的嬰兒
a **swimming** boy　正在游泳的男孩	a **weeping** child　一個哭泣的孩子

► The **closing** scene of the play was a very sad one. 這齣戲的最後一幕很令人難過。

► The **drowning** boy flung out his hands wildly. 這個溺水的男孩瘋也似地揮舞著雙手。

► We were discussing the **interesting** film we had seen.

我們正在討論我們看過的那部有趣影片。

► They are known as a **dancing** couple. 他們以舞壇情侶而聞名。

► We laughed at the end of his **amusing** story. 聽完他的有趣故事，我們笑了。

► **Barking** dogs seldom bite. 會叫的狗不咬人。

► It was a **thrilling** game, and we enjoyed it very much.

那是一個很刺激的遊戲，我們愛死它了。

► The sound of **running** water nearby gave us hope. 附近的流水聲給了我們希望。

► The **increasing** number of accidents alarmed him. 節節上升的車禍次數使他恐懼不安。

過去分詞

a **wounded** soldier 一名傷兵	a **spoiled** child 一個被寵壞的孩子
a **stolen** article 被偷的物品	a **broken** promise 被違背的諾言
the **fried** fish 炸魚	a **hunted** animal 被獵捕的動物

► She picked up the **broken** pieces of glass. 她把玻璃碎片撿起來。

► The **wounded** animal disappeared into the forest. 這隻受傷的動物消失在森林裡。

► The **frightened** boy let out a loud scream. 受到驚嚇的男孩大聲尖叫。

► Even after all these years, no one could find the **lost** treasure.

即使多年以後，還是沒人能找到這失落的寶藏。

► She mended the **torn** dress. 她縫補這件被扯破的洋裝。

► The **escaped** convict has been caught again. 那個逃犯已再次被捕。

► We threw away all our **tattered** clothes. 我們把所有破衣服都扔掉了。

► The **amused** audience burst into laughter. 被逗樂的觀眾突然大笑。

(c) 現在分詞和過去分詞都可以放在感官動詞（如 see、smell、taste、feel、watch、hear 等）的受詞之後，作受詞補語，兩者意義不同。現在分詞具有主動、進行的涵義；過去分詞則有被動、完成的涵義。

USAGE PRACTICE

現在分詞

基礎文法寶典❹
Essential English Usage & Grammar

▶ We saw her **hurrying** to catch the bus. 我們看見她急著去趕車。

▶ I saw him **breaking** the lock. 我看見他撬開鎖。

▶ She saw him **climbing** up the tree. 她看著他爬上樹。

▶ I felt somebody **watching** me. 我感覺有人在看著我。

▶ He felt something **creeping** down his arm. 他感覺有東西爬下他的手臂。

▶ I smelled the food **burning**. 我聞到食物燒焦了。

▶ He noticed the boy **behaving** in a furtive manner. 他注意到這個男孩舉止鬼鬼祟祟。

▶ They heard someone **shouting** for help. 他們聽到有人喊救命。

▶ We watched the workmen **digging** up the road. 我們看著工人挖馬路。

過去分詞

▶ We would like to see the place **locked** up at night. 我們希望這個地方在晚上是鎖上的。

▶ I like to see her **dressed** up in white lace. 我喜歡看她盛裝穿著白色蕾絲的衣服。

▶ I saw him **held** tightly in the grasp of the policeman. 我看見他被警察緊緊地抓住。

▶ He did not watch the game **played** by the school team. 他沒看校隊的比賽。

▶ We watched the play **performed** on stage. 我們觀賞舞台上演出的戲劇。

 分詞還可以當作其他不完全及物動詞的受詞補語，如 find、want、imagine 或使役動詞（have、make 等）；現在分詞仍然表示「主動或進行」，過去分詞則表示「被動或完成」。

▶ We were pleased to find him **working** hard. 我們很高興發現他正努力工作。

▶ We found him **lying** unconscious in his bedroom.
我們發現他不省人事地躺在他的臥室裡。

▶ They wanted the same song **played** over and over again.
他們要同一首歌一遍又一遍地被播放。

▶ I could imagine her **making** a fool of herself. 我可以想像她自己出醜。

▶ We had bananas **fried** with flour. 我們把香蕉裹著麵粉去炸。

請根據提示在空格中填入正確的分詞形式。

1. We looked helplessly at the _____ (*burn*) house.

2. The film that we saw last night was most _____ (*bore*).

3. The _____ (*depress*) man felt like killing himself.

4. He stepped on a piece of _____ (*break*) bottle and cut his foot.

5. The language _____ (*speak*) here is a mixture of Spanish and Urdu.

6. The glorious sunset is always an _____ (*inspire*) sight.

7. The woman lifted the _____ (*cry*) baby and rocked it in her arms.

8. I saw the children _____ (*play*) at the playground.

9. I was glad to find my students _____ (*read*) quietly in the library.

10. He looked at me fearfully, like a _____ (*frighten*) animal.

11. I felt something _____ (*crawl*) up my leg.

12. That old seaman told us a most _____ (*amaze*) story last night.

13. A _____ (*grow*) child needs adequate food and sufficient hours of sleep.

14. He was _____ (*heartbreak*) to find his house _____ (*burn*) down to the ground.

15. The _____ (*escape*) convict was surrounded by the police.

☞ 更多相關習題請見本章應用練習 Part 1。

16-2 現在分詞與動名詞

(a) 現在分詞與動名詞都是由動詞字尾加 ing 構成，容易混淆。一般而言，須從用法上分辨兩者：動名詞帶有名詞性，可以修飾名詞，表示該名詞的「用途」；而現在分詞則帶有形容詞性，也可以修飾名詞，表示該名詞的「狀態」。另外，現在分詞與動名詞修飾名詞時的讀法是不同的，前者重音在名詞上，後者的重音則在動名詞本身上。

USAGE PRACTICE	
動名詞	現在分詞
a **walking** stick 手杖 （用來支持人走路的手杖）	a **walking** doll 正在行走的洋娃娃
a **running** board （早期汽車兩旁的）腳踏板 （讓人踏著下車用的踏板）	**running** water 流動的水
a **sleeping** car （火車）臥車 （用來讓乘客睡覺的車廂）	a **sleeping** child 正在睡覺的小孩
a **fitting** room 試衣間 （用來給顧客試穿衣服的房間）	a **fitting** speech 適當的演講
a **traveling** bag 旅行袋	a **traveling** circus 巡迴馬戲團

基礎文法寶典 ❹
Essential English Usage & Grammar

（讓人旅行用的袋子）

▶ **Walking** is a good form of exercise.
走路是一種好運動。

▶ I scolded some boys for **kicking** a dog.
我責罵一些男孩，因為他們踢狗。

▶ **Singing** is one of my hobbies.
唱歌是我的嗜好之一。

▶ The woman **walking** toward us is my
aunt. 朝我們走來的女人是我的阿姨。

▶ I saw some boys **kicking** a dog.
我看見一些男孩在踢一隻狗。

▶ The girl **singing** now is my sister.
現在正在唱歌的女孩是我的妹妹。

16-3 分詞片語的位置及用法

(a) 關係子句可以簡化成分詞片語，置於名詞之後作為修飾。簡化的步驟是：
    (1) 省略關係代名詞。
    (2) 將表示「主動」的動詞改為現在分詞、表示「進行」的動詞刪掉 be 動詞並保
        留現在分詞、表示「被動」的動詞刪掉 be 動詞並保留過去分詞。

USAGE PRACTICE

▶ The book **belonging** (= that belongs) to her sister has been found.
這本屬於她的姊姊的書已經被找到了。

▶ The only road **leading** (= that leads) to the town is under floodwaters.
通往城裡唯一的道路被淹沒了。

▶ Look at the bird **perching** (= which perches) on the branch. 看那隻停在樹枝上的鳥。

▶ The woman **selling** (= who sells) vegetables is a widow. 賣蔬菜的女人是個寡婦。

▶ The old lady **wearing** (= who is wearing) the hat is my neighbor.
那位戴著帽子的老太太是我的鄰居。

▶ That boy **coming** (= who is coming) toward us is Kenneth's cousin.
那個朝我們走過來的男孩是肯尼士的表兄弟。

▶ The boy **cycling** (= who is cycling) toward the post office is my brother.
正騎單車往郵局去的男孩是我的弟弟。

▶ That is the tourist **seeking** (= who is seeking) information on those ancient temples.
那位就是在找尋古寺資料的遊客。

▶ The men **hunting** (= who are hunting) the escaped tiger are from the Zoo Authorities.

追捕逃脫的老虎的那些人來於自動物園當局。

▶ They took pictures of the car **damaged** (= which was damaged) in the accident.

他們為在車禍中受損的車子拍照。

▶ His favorite dish is chicken **fried** (= which is fried) with potatoes.

他最喜歡的菜是雞肉炒馬鈴薯。

▶ She likes food **cooked** (= which is cooked) this way. 她喜歡以這種方法烹煮的食物。

▶ They brought home the soldier **wounded** (= who was wounded) in the ambush.

他們把在埋伏戰中受傷的士兵帶回家。

 分詞片語的位置考量必須格外謹慎，應該盡可能靠近要修飾的字詞，以免造成意思上的混淆不清。

▶ He saw a monkey **swinging** from tree to tree. → O

他看到一隻猴子在樹間盪來盪去。（分詞片語放在名詞 monkey 後，加以修飾）

▶ **Swinging** from tree to tree, he saw a monkey. → X

（分詞片語放在句首修飾 he，意思上變成「他」在樹間盪來盪去）

▶ They found the treasure chest **covered** by the weeds. → O

他們發現這個被雜草覆蓋的藏寶箱。（分詞片語放在名詞 the treasure chest 後，加以修飾）

▶ **Covered** by the weeds, they found the treasure chest. → X

（分詞片語放在句首修飾 they，意思上變成「他們」被雜草覆蓋）

小練習

請根據提示在空格中填入正確的分詞形式。

1. The man _____ (*stand*) beside the car is my uncle.

2. The dress _____ (*wear*) by Jill's cousin to the party costs over fifty dollars.

3. The smoke _____ (*come*) from the burning houses was thick and black.

4. The priceless vase _____ (*steal*) by the thief twenty years ago has never been found.

5. The flag _____ (*fly*) in front of the school is faded and torn.

6. Who is going to clean up all the mess _____ (*make*) by those who came to the party?

7. The students _____ (*talk*) at the back of the class seldom pay attention to the teacher.

8. I found a secret door _____ (*lead*) to the treasure room.

9. These animals, _____ (*hunt*) down by trappers for their fur, have been decreasing in number over the years.

10. Go and see if the clothes _____ (*hang*) outside are already dry.

11. The teacher warned that any student not _____ (*hand*) in his homework on time would be punished.

12. Can't you hear him _____ (*sing*) at the top of his voice in the other room?

13. There's someone _____ (*sleep*) on the couch. Shall we wake him up?

14. The man _____ (*water*) the plants is my uncle.

15. The children do not like vegetables _____ (*cook*) in soup.

16-4 分詞構句的位置及用法

(a) 可以將表示「時間」、「原因」等意思的副詞子句和表示「連續或附帶狀況」的對等子句簡化為分詞構句。簡化的步驟是：

(1) 省略引導副詞子句或對等子句的連接詞。

(2) 省略副詞子句或對等子句的主詞。

(3) 將表示「主動」的動詞改為現在分詞、表示「進行」的動詞刪掉 be 動詞並保留現在分詞、表示「被動」的動詞刪掉 be 動詞並保留過去分詞。

(4) 分詞構句可以在主要子句的前面、後面或中間，通常用逗號隔開。注意，子句與主句的主詞須指涉同一人。

USAGE PRACTICE

表示原因

▶ **Being** (= As she was) naturally curious, she listened at the keyhole.
由於天生好奇心強，她在鑰匙孔邊偷聽。

▶ **Thinking** (= Since I thought) that she was safe with them, I did not bother to call.
因為認為她和他們在一起很安全，我就不特地打電話。

▶ **Standing** (= Since he stood) by the doorway, he could see everything going on.
由於站在出入口旁邊，他可以看見一切正在進行的事物。

▶ She wore a sleeveless dress, **thinking** (= because she thought) that it was going to be a hot day. 她以為天氣會很熱，所以穿無袖的衣服。

▶ **Not realizing** (= Because I didn't realize) its significance, I paid little attention to it.
因為不瞭解它的重要性，我沒有注意它。（簡化否定句時須保留否定詞 not）

▶ **Shocked** (= As they were shocked) by his rude behavior, they did not know what to do.

因為被他的粗魯行為嚇了一大跳，他們不知所措。

▶ **Frightened** (= Since she was frightened) by the dog, she refused to open the gate.

因為被那隻狗嚇壞了，她拒絕打開大門。

▶ We went to bed early, **exhausted** (= because we were exhausted) by the long journey.

因為長途旅行而筋疲力盡，我們早早就寢。

▶ He knocked down the man, **determined** (= since he was determined) not to let him get away. 因為決心不讓他逃走，他把那個人擊倒。

▶ **Angered** (= Since he was angered) by her refusal to help him, he left the house.

他向她求助遭拒，憤而離開房子。

▶ **Weakened** (= Since he was weakened) by his prolonged illness, he could not get out of bed. 由於久病而虛弱，他無法下床。

▶ She looked at him strangely, **puzzled** (= because she was puzzled) by the question he had asked. 她訝異地看著他，因為對他的問題感到困惑。

▶ **Bound** (= Since he was bound) with strong ropes, he could not move.

由於被堅固的繩索綁著，他無法移動。

▶ She ran out of the room, **hurt** (= because she was hurt) by his insult.

因為被他的侮辱所傷害，她從房間跑了出去。

▶ **Shocked** (= As she was shocked) by the news, she fainted.

她被這消息所震驚，就昏倒了。

表示時間

▶ **Examining** (= While he was examining) the specimen with care, he discovered something. 當他正小心地檢查這個標本的時候，發現了某件東西。

▶ **Driving** (= When we drove) toward town, we saw an accident.

開車去鎮上的時候，我們目睹了一場意外。

▶ **Running** (= While he was running) down the path, he tripped over a stone.

跑下小徑時，他被一塊石頭絆倒。

▶ **Standing** (= When we stood) on the hill, we could see the whole town.

站在山丘上時，我們能看見整個鎮。

表示連續或附帶狀況

▶ I strolled along the road, **hoping** (= and I hoped) to meet her. 我沿路閒逛，希望能遇見她。

▶ He turned his head quickly, **pretending** (= and he pretended) not to have seen anything.

他很快地轉頭，假裝什麼都沒看見。

▶ He is out in the field, **practicing** (= and he practiced) for the match tomorrow.

他人在球場，為明天的比賽練習。

▶ We went into the shop, **intending** (= and we intended) to buy some books.

我們走進店內，想要買一些書。

▶ I walked onto the stage, **hoping** (= and I hoped) I wouldn't be too nervous.

我走上台，暗自希望我不會太緊張。

▶ **He** walked up and down the platform, **looking** (= and he looked) at his watch.

他在月台上來回走著，看著他的手錶。

▶ The boys are in the field, **flying** (= and they are flying) kites.　男孩們在運動場上放風箏。

▶ They are on the highway now, **approaching** (= and they are approaching) the tunnel.

他們現在在高速公路上，接近隧道了。

▶ She is in the room, **sewing** (= and she is sewing) a dress.　她在房間裡縫衣服。

▶ His father was sitting outside, **smoking** (= and he was smoking) a pipe.

他父親坐在外面，抽著煙斗。

▶ He pushed the thought out of his head, **determined** (= and he was determined) not to let it worry him.　他將這個念頭拋諸腦後，決心不讓它來煩自己。

▶ I let out a big sigh, **relieved** (= and I was relieved) that the examination was all over.

我呼出一大口氣，感到考完試如釋重負。

▶ We all hastened to congratulate him, **delighted** (= and we were delighted) that he had won the contest.　我們都急著去向他道賀，很高興他贏得了比賽。

▶ There she is, **talking** (= and she was talking) to her friends.

她在那裡，正和她的朋友講話。

 分詞構句的位置考量必須格外謹慎，應該盡可能靠近要修飾的字詞，以免造成意思上的混淆不清。

▶ **Riding** across the field, the man saw a large number of the dead. → O
騎過田野時，這男人看到很多死人。（分詞構句放在主詞 the man 前，加以修飾）

▶ The man saw a large number of the dead, **riding** across the field. → X
（死人不會騎車，分詞構句放在名詞 the dead 後作修飾是錯誤的）

▶ **Glancing** out of the window, I could see a car. → O
從窗戶看出去，我能看到一輛車。（分詞構句放在主詞 I 前，加以修飾）
▶ **Glancing** out of the window, a car could be seen. → X
（必須是人才能從窗戶看出去，不可能是車子，分詞構句放在主詞 a car 前做修飾是錯誤的）
▶ **Strolling** in the garden, I saw some lovely flowers. → O
在花園中散步時，我看見一些美麗的花。（分詞構句放在主詞 I 前，加以修飾）
▶ I saw some lovely flowers, **strolling** in the garden. → X
（花不會散步，分詞構句放在名詞 flowers 後做修飾是錯誤的）

小練習

請根據提示在空格中填入正確的分詞形式。

1. _____ (*feel*) hungry, the tiger went to hunt for food.

2. Badly _____ (*injure*) in the accident, the passengers were taken to the hospital.

3. _____ (*squat*) down, he tied his shoelaces.

4. His father could not concentrate on the paper, _____ (*disturb*) by all the noise the children were making.

5. _____ (*think*) that he couldn't trust her, he delivered the message himself.

6. _____ (*stand*) on the hill, we had a splendid view of the whole town.

7. Peter and Paul are outside, _____ (*play*) baseball in the garden.

8. _____ (*hear*) a loud scream for help, we rushed outside into the street.

9. We came as early as possible, _____ (*try*) to get front seats.

10. _____ (*watch*) him eat all those chicken and ham sandwiches, I felt hungry, too.

11. _____ (*frighten*) at the sight of the accident, he did not know what to do.

12. _____ (*manage*) to save the lives of two civilians, the soldier lost his own life.

13. _____ (*exhaust*), he slept like a log the whole night.

14. _____ (*climb*) over the wall, the thief was caught by the police.

15. _____ (*anger*) by his refusal, they stomped out.

16. My brother is in his room, _____ (*read*) a book.

17. He slammed the door, _____ (*annoy*) at what they had done.

18. _____ (*astonish*) by the look on her face, I rushed to help her.

19. My uncle is in his study, _____ (*write*) a letter.

20. _____ (*startle*) in the act of prying, he could only mutter some silly excuses.

基礎文法寶典❹
Essential English Usage & Grammar

21. _____ (*determine*) never to give up, he tried again.

16-5 分詞的時態和語態

(a) 以下是用 do 為例，列出分詞的各種時態與語態。因為過去分詞本身就是構成完成式和被動語態的要素，所以沒有另外的完成式形態，也沒有主動的用法。

	現在分詞		過去分詞
	簡單式	完成式	簡單式
主　動	doing	having done	
被　動	being done	having been done	done

(b) 不論在分詞構句還是分詞片語中，完成式的現在分詞表示「在主要動詞前發生或已完成的動作」，而現在分詞簡單式被動語態中的 being 可以省略。

USAGE PRACTICE

▶ **Having done** (= Since she had done) this before, she knew what to do.

　因為以前已經做過這件事，她知道該怎樣處理。

▶ **Having eaten** (= After it had eaten) a heavy meal, the python could only move very sluggishly. 吃了豐盛的一餐後，蟒蛇只能很緩慢地移動。

▶ **Having visited** (= Since she has visited) the place before, she does not want to go again.

　因為以前已經參觀過這個地方，她不想再去一次。

▶ **Having waited** for an hour (= After we had waited for an hour), we went off without her.

　等了一小時之後，我們不等她就離開。

▶ **Having finished** his work (= After he had finished his work), he did not know what to do next. 完成工作以後，他不知道接下來該做什麼。

▶ I was very tired, **having worked** (= because I had worked) hard the whole day.

　努力工作一天後，我感覺非常疲倦。

▶ We were not interested in the story, **having heard** (= because we had heard) it before.

　我們對這個故事不感興趣，因為我們以前就聽過了。

▶ **Having promised** (= As I had promised) to be on time, I hurried to keep the appointment.

　因為已經答應會準時到，我匆忙去赴約。

▶ **Having been warned** (= Since he had been warned) not to play near the swamp, he kept as far away from it as possible.

因為曾經被人警告不要在沼澤附近玩耍，他儘可能地遠離那個地方。

注意 簡化成分詞構句或分詞片語時，否定詞 (not、never) 要保留，並且要放到現在分詞之前。

▶ **Not having seen** (= Since I had not seen) her for a long time, I paid her a visit.
因為已經很久沒有看見她，我去拜訪她。

▶ She didn't know what to do, **not having been** (= because she had not been) in such a situation before. 因為以前從未遇過這樣的情形，所以她不知道該怎麼做。

▶ **Not having been informed** (= As he hadn't been informed) about the change in plans, he did not know what to do. 計畫有變卻沒人告知他，他因而不知所措。

▶ The boy, **never having met** (= who had never met) such wealthy people before, looked at them with awe. 這男孩從未見過這樣的有錢人，他敬畏地注視著他們。

▶ **Never having seen** (= Since I had never seen) such a thing before, I was very interested.
因為以前從未看過這樣的事情，我感到很有興趣。

▶ **Never having been** (= As she had never been) there before, she decided to go.
因為以前沒去過那裡，她決定要去。

▶ Peggy was very nervous, **never having been operated** (= because she had never been operated) on before. 佩姬很焦慮，因為她從來沒有動過手術。

▶ **Having written** and (having) **sent** the letter, I could only wait for the reply.
寫好信也把它寄出去之後，我只能等待回音了。

▶ **Never having been taught** or (having been) **told** what to say on such occasions, she was dumbfounded.
由於從來沒有人教她或告訴她在這樣的一些場合該說什麼，她目瞪口呆。

★當一個句子使用兩個完成式的分詞時，第二個分詞的 having 可以省略。

小練習
請根據提示在空格中填入正確的完成式分詞構句。

1. _____ (*not/hear*) from them for a long time, I decided to call them.

2. _____ (*forget*) to lock the gate, I turned back to do so.

3. _____ (*promise*) to return early, I stayed there for only half an hour.

4. _____ (*convince*) himself it was all right, he signed the document.

5. _____ (*punish*) for chewing shoes once, the dog never chewed our shoes again.

基礎文法寶典❹
Essential English Usage & Grammar

6. We felt more at ease, _____ (*assure*) that someone would be at the airport to meet us.

7. _____ (*never/be*) on an airplane before, the twins felt very nervous at first.

8. He was not allowed to go out, _____ (*not/recover*) fully from his illness yet.

9. _____ (*sprain*) his ankle, the boy had to go slowly.

10. _____ (*not/see*) my cousin for such a long time, I was surprised at how tall he had grown.

11. _____ nearly _____ (*kill*) in a trap once before, the mouse was very careful to avoid this one.

12. _____ (*not/inform*) about the meeting, Thomas did not turn up on Saturday.

13. _____ (*find*) what he wanted, he was content to sit and wait for us.

14. _____ (*never/hear*) about the iPhone before, the child was most surprised to see one in the room.

15. _____ (*learn*) that they were only his adoptive parents, he set out to find his real ones.

16. _____ (*clear*) off the table and _____ (*wash*) the plates, she cleaned up the kitchen.

17. _____ (*not/do*) my homework or_____ (*practice*) on the piano yet, I refused to go out with them.

18. _____ (*lock*) all the doors and _____ (*shut*) all the windows, he went to bed.

19. I did not know where my friend lived,_____ (*never/be*) to her house before.

20. _____ (*scold*) once already, the boys dared not approach him again.

21. They were all rather bored by the tale, _____ (*hear*) it many times before.

16-6 獨立分詞構句

(a) 當分詞構句的主詞與主要子句的主詞不同時，兩個主詞皆須保留，以免造成意義上的混淆，這類用法稱為獨立分詞構句。

USAGE PRACTICE
▶ **This done,** we loaded the goods onto the truck. 做完這件事，我們把這批貨物裝到貨車上。

> ▶ We ventured into the jungle, **Paul taking** the lead. 由保羅領隊，我們冒險進入叢林。
>
> ▶ **Today being** a holiday, the offices are all closed. 今天是假日，辦公室全都沒開。

Chapter 16　應用練習

PART 1

請根據提示在空格中填入正確的分詞形式。

1. A _____ (roll) stone gathers no moss.

2. We have had the fence _____ (mend) so that the goats won't be able to enter the garden.

3. She went into the kitchen just in time to take the _____ (boil) kettle off the stove.

4. She swept together all the _____ (break) pieces of glass and threw them away.

5. They watched him _____ (do) cartwheels on the lawn.

6. The boys started digging holes everywhere in the compound in their search for _____ (hide) treasure.

7. We saw her _____ (lie) unconscious on the floor.

8. They found a large crowd _____ (gather) in front of the movie theater.

9. Look! Can you see the bird _____ (perch) on the fence over there?

10. The _____ (amuse) audience roared with laughter as they watched the _____ (amuse) actor staggering about on the stage and singing at the top of his voice.

11. We saw them _____ (run) down the road as fast as they could in order to catch the bus.

12. You must bring along your _____ (travel) suit when we go to the seaside.

13. Even an _____ (experience) man would not do such a risky thing, so you who don't have any experience at all should not try it.

14. The _____ (frighten) child refused to go into the room.

15. She heard somebody _____ (scream) for help.

16. We want this piece of work _____ (finish) by tomorrow.

PART 2

請利用分詞（分詞形容詞、分詞片語或分詞構句）來合併以下的句子。

1. Is there somebody upstairs? He is playing the harmonica.

$\rightarrow$ _____

2. The dress was trimmed with red ribbons and lace. The dress looked very attractive.

   $\rightarrow$ _____

3. Tomorrow, there will be another bus. It will take you to school.

   $\rightarrow$ _____

4. The bride had a long, lace veil. It had been worn by her mother at her wedding years ago.

   $\rightarrow$ _____

5. We noticed some men. They were digging up the road.

   $\rightarrow$ _____

6. He doesn't know the facts. He finds it hard to give an answer.

   $\rightarrow$ _____

7. The team was losing in the first half of the game. They pledged to do their best to win in the second half.

   $\rightarrow$ _____

8. The tennis racket was stolen by someone several days ago. It was recovered by my friend today.

   $\rightarrow$ _____

9. The signboard is broken. It is hanging outside the shop.

   $\rightarrow$ _____

10. The spare parts were needed urgently. They were flown in from the United States.

    $\rightarrow$ _____

11. The soldiers were approaching. They tried to launch a surprise attack.

    $\rightarrow$ _____

12. This is the brochure. It gives you all the information on the district.

    $\rightarrow$ _____

13. The boys were exhausted. They refused to walk any further.

    $\rightarrow$ _____

14. The school principal admired the painting. It was painted by the art students.

    $\rightarrow$ _____

15. He walked into the garden. He was whistling loudly.

    $\rightarrow$ _____

16. The room was cleaned at the beginning of the week. It was dirty again at the end of the week.

→ _____

17. She looked at the trees in the distance. They were swaying in the strong wind.

→ _____

18. The three passengers were injured in the accident. They were taken to the hospital.

→ _____

19. The essay was written by him. It won first prize in the competition.

→ _____

20. Don't step on the mousetrap. It is lying in the doorway.

→ _____

PART 3

請利用分詞（分詞形容詞、分詞片語或分詞構句）來合併以下的句子。

1. We watched the fishermen. They were throwing nets into the sea.

→ _____

2. The boys is my brother. He is taking the salute in the march past.

→ _____

3. She recognized the man. He was wanted for murder by the police.

→ _____

4. We found him. He was hiding under the bed.

→ _____

5. She took all the money. The money was kept in the safe.

→ _____

6. She went to the dinner. She thought it would be over in two hours.

→ _____

7. The police fired tear gas. They hoped to frighten away the mob.

→ _____

8. The car was damaged beyond repair. It was parked by the side of the road.

→ _____

9. The book was bound in a hard cover. It belonged to my mother.

→ _____

10. My brother is in the garden. He is trimming the hedge.

→ _____

11. The purse was lost during the game. It has been found by one of the spectators.

→ _____

12. We were assisted by Mr. Lewis. We managed to complete the project.

→ _____

13. My sister touched the pot. She did not realize that it was hot.

→ _____

14. I accidentally stepped into a hole. It had been dug for the purpose of planting a tree.

→ _____

15. We walked up and down the room. We tried to find a way to solve our problem.

→ _____

16. The driver lost control of his car. He hit a pedestrian and smashed into a shop window.

→ _____

17. The boy was carried out by some members of the St. John's Ambulance Brigade. He had been hurt during the rugby game.

→ _____

18. We saw a beautiful painting. It was placed in a big, carved frame.

→ _____

19. Here is the notice. It tells me that I have been dismissed from the firm.

→ _____

PART 4

請利用分詞（分詞形容詞、分詞片語或分詞構句）來合併以下的句子。

1. The boy stood on the shore. He watched the fishermen. They were casting their nets into the sea.

→ _____

2. Did you see a man with a long beard? He passed this way a few minutes ago.

→ _____

3. The essay was written by one of my classmates. It won first prize in the competition.

→ _____

分　詞
Chapter 16

4. The child was lost in the crowd. She cried with fright.

→ _____

5. They chased away the young man. They did not know that he was their own son.

→ _____

6. He was exhausted at the end of the day. He had a very good night's sleep.

→ _____

7. Peter got out of bed slowly. He thought that there was plenty of time for him to get ready.

→ _____

8. The children heard the bell of the ice-cream man. They rushed out to stop him.

→ _____

9. They were discussing an article in the newspaper. It was written by a young lecturer.

→ _____

10. He set out when it became dark. He thought that he could travel unseen at night.

→ _____

11. Many people stood on the beach. They watched the life guard rescue the girl. She was drowning.

→ _____

12. He was trapped in the small room. He could not move at all.

→ _____

13. They stared at the huge animal. It was blocking their path.

→ _____

14. Here is a booklet. It gives some information of the most famous tourist attractions in the country.

→ _____

15. Do you see something? It is moving in the water.

→ _____

16. She got on the bus. She did not realize it was the wrong one.

→ _____

17. I picked up the phone to call him. I wondered whether he had reached home.

→ _____

PART 5

請利用分詞（分詞形容詞、分詞片語或分詞構句）來合併以下的句子。

1. He closed the door with a bang. He strode angrily into the room.

   → _____

2. I noticed two men. They were lurking furtively near the jewelry shop.

   → _____

3. He thought it was the right time. He put forward his suggestions to them.

   → _____

4. She decided that the dress could not be mended again. It was torn and tattered.

   → _____

5. The teacher was in the staff room. He was grading some exercise books.

   → _____

6. Did you happen to notice a black car? It passed this way a few minutes ago.

   → _____

7. There was a tractor. It was leveling the ground.

   → _____

8. The detective examined the room thoroughly. He hoped to find some clue to the mysterious happenings.

   → _____

9. I did not know his real intention. I did as he suggested.

   → _____

10. I flipped the case open. I got a very big shock.

    → _____

11. Here is the page. It gives a description of the chief character in the book.

    → _____

12. She pretended not to notice him. She walked to a side stall and stood there. She looked at some magazines.

    → _____

PART 6

請利用分詞（分詞形容詞、分詞片語或分詞構句）來合併以下的句子。

1. There they are. They are listening to the band.

→ _____

2. He saw an accident. He was riding to school.

→ _____

3. The girl was deserted by her family and friends. She ran away to another village.

→ _____

4. He was running into the garden. He tripped over a brick.

→ _____

5. He was stunned by the blow. He slumped to the ground unconsciously.

→ _____

6. He is in the garden. He is practicing the art of self-defense.

→ _____

7. I did not hear the song. It was played on the radio.

→ _____

8. She is in the backyard. She is putting out the clothes to dry.

→ _____

9. My friend is in London. He is taking a course in business administration.

→ _____

10. The beggar slept on the sidewalk. He had no home to go to.

→ _____

11. He looked at the hysterical woman. He wondered what had happened.

→ _____

12. She thought of the days ahead. She hoped that everything would go well for her.

→ _____

13. He did not know what to do. He was chased by the angry bull.

→ _____

14. He has lost the book. It contains an informative account of life in the Pacific Islands.

→ _____

15. She ran out of the room. She was embarrassed by what he had said.

→ _____

PART 7

請利用分詞（分詞形容詞、分詞片語或分詞構句）來合併以下的句子。

1. When we stood on the balcony, we could see the whole park.

   → _____

2. The old man was limping across the road because he had been knocked down by a taxi.

   → _____

3. When we were walking through the park, we saw some oak trees.

   → _____

4. Since my father was stunned by the news, he could find no words to say.

   → _____

5. He tripped over the bucket which contained water.

   → _____

6. Because he was disgusted by what he saw, he averted his face.

   → _____

7. He saw the farmer who was setting fire to the barn.

   → _____

8. The scuba divers found the wrecked launch which was covered with weeds.

   → _____

9. As Alan saw that it was raining, he looked around for his raincoat.

   → _____

10. Since the dog was securely tied to the tree, it could only bark at the stranger.

   → _____

11. Because she was born and bred in the country, she was bewildered by the sights in the city.

   → _____

12. She hid her face in her hands as she was terrified by what she had seen.

   → _____

13. After my work was all completed, I could get ready to go home.

   → _____

14. The concert, which was staged by the kindergarten children, was a great success.

   → _____

15. She tossed and turned in bed, and she was thinking of the bleak future ahead.

→ _____

16. Since Christmas is a holiday, we don't need to go to the office.

→ _____

17. We crossed the mountainous border, and Malcolm acted as a guide.

→ _____

PART 8

請利用分詞（分詞形容詞、分詞片語或分詞構句）來合併以下的句子。

1. As he was feeling sleepy, he went to bed early.

→ _____

2. Since we had finished our work, we were allowed to have a short break.

→ _____

3. I saw the actors who were preparing themselves for the final scene.

→ _____

4. As we were riding along the track, we saw an old man walking with a stick.

→ _____

5. The soldiers who were trained by this captain were very good fighters.

→ _____

6. After he had washed the car, the boy wiped the windscreen.

→ _____

7. I saw the lifeguard who was rescuing the swimmer.

→ _____

8. We did not leave the house as we had been told not to do so.

→ _____

9. Because the villagers had been warned of the enemy's approach, they set up barricades outside the village.

→ _____

10. As he saw that the weather was fine, he went out for a walk.

→ _____

11. Since the construction workers had worked at tall buildings before, they did not feel dizzy at all.

→ _____

12. The man who was wanted by the police escaped to another country.

→ _____

13. As he was determined to pass his examination, he studied very hard.

→ _____

14. The children do not like fish that is cooked that way.

→ _____

15. As he drove through the countryside, he saw fields of corn.

→ _____

16. As she is a sensitive person, she is easily hurt.

→ _____

17. The woman who is giving away the prizes is the wife of the mayor.

→ _____

18. The boys who are teasing the newcomer were told off roundly by the teacher.

→ _____

PART 9

請利用分詞（分詞形容詞、分詞片語或分詞構句）來合併以下的句子。

1. As he had seen the movie before, he did not want to go.

→ _____

2. The guests who were sitting in the big tent had a great view of the sports events.

→ _____

3. When he was hurrying to catch a bus, Terry tripped over a log.

→ _____

4. As she was astonished at what she had heard, she did not know what to say.

→ _____

5. I can see the dog which is chewing a bone.

→ _____

6. As he was disappointed with his results, he vowed to do better.

→ _____

7. As I did not know how to do the work, I left it alone.

→ _____

8. As she searched through an old chest, she found some old but valuable stamps.

→ _____

9. When the policeman saw an old woman who was crossing a busy road, he rushed to her aid.

→ _____

10. He never did the trick again, as he had been warned by the headmaster.

→ _____

11. Since he was exhausted by the journey, he did not mind where he slept.

→ _____

12. As she thought over a past amusing incident, she laughed out loud.

→ _____

13. Since he was not angry with her anymore, he spoke to her again.

→ _____

基礎文法寶典 ❹
Essential English Usage & Grammar

Chapter 17 一致性

17-1 單數主詞接單數動詞的情況

	be 動詞	助動詞 do	助動詞 have	一般動詞現在式
第一人稱 (I)	am/was	do/did	have/had	原形
第二人稱 (you)	are/were	do/did	have/had	原形
第三人稱 (it, he, she, his friend, the driver...)	is/was	does/did	has/had	字尾加上 s

(a) 主詞為單數時，要依人稱使用正確的單數動詞或單數助動詞。

USAGE PRACTICE

▶ I **am** not feeling well tonight. 我今晚覺得不太舒服。

▶ I **am** going to the library this afternoon. 今天下午我要去圖書館。

▶ I **was** delayed by the traffic yesterday. 昨天我因為交通而被耽擱。

▶ I **don't** like butter, but I **like** cheese. 我不喜歡奶油，但我喜歡乳酪。

▶ I **have** sold ten books of coupons. 我已經賣了十本優待卷。（have 是助動詞）

▶ She **comes** and **goes** as she **likes**. 她隨自己喜歡來去自如。

▶ She **is** going to Paris tomorrow. 她明天要去巴黎。

▶ She **is** at a hair salon now. 她現在在美髮店。

▶ She **does** her work efficiently. 她的工作效率很高。（does 是一般動詞）

▶ **Does** she walk home every day? 她每天走路回家嗎？（does 是助動詞）

▶ He **was** at home all yesterday afternoon. 他昨天一整個下午都在家。

▶ He **has** a cherry tree in his garden. 他的花園裡有一棵櫻桃樹。（has 是一般動詞）

▶ His horse **has** won first place. 他的馬贏得第一名。（has 是助動詞）

▶ The dog **was** not pleased at being tied up. 這隻狗因為被綁起來而不高興。

(b) 不可數名詞作主詞時，後接單數動詞或單數助動詞。

USAGE PRACTICE

▶ Salt **is** the seasoning that most people cannot do without.

鹽是大部份人不可或缺的調味料。

▶ Oil **has** made Saudi Arabia a rich country. 石油已經讓沙烏地阿拉伯成為一個富有的國家。

▶ Milk **contains** all the necessary nutritious elements. 牛奶含有所有必需的營養素。

▶ Some sugar **has** been added to sweeten it. 已經加了一些糖使它變甜。

▶ Air **is** a mixture of gases. 空氣是多種氣體的混合物。

▶ Wood **is** useful for many purposes. 木材有許多用途。

▶ The food **is** already cold. 這食物已經冷掉了。

▶ All the money which she had in the purse **was** stolen. 她皮包裡所有的錢都被偷了。

▶ The information you gave me **is** not enough. 你給我的資訊不夠充足。

(c) 抽象名詞作主詞時，後接單數動詞或單數助動詞。

USAGE PRACTICE

▶ Justice **forbids** the abuse of laws. 司法禁止法律濫用。

▶ His advice **was** always heeded by the students. 他的忠告總是被學生所注意。

▶ Your behavior **is** unpardonable. 你的行為是不可寬恕的。

▶ The laughter of the boys **was** distinctly clear. 男孩們的笑聲清晰嘹亮。

(d) 不定代名詞 anybody、anything、anyone、someone、somebody、something、
everything、everybody、everyone、nobody、nothing、no one 等是單數名詞，
作主詞時，要用單數動詞或單數助動詞。

USAGE PRACTICE

▶ Everybody **is** at home today. 今天每一個人都在家。

▶ Everyone **has** his own faults. 每人有他自己的缺點。

▶ Everything **has** been arranged. Nothing **is** out of place.
一切都已安排妥當，沒有東西不是各就其位的。

▶ Someone **has** taken something that **is** very valuable. 有人拿走某個很有價值的東西。

▶ **Does** anybody know where he lives? 有任何人知道他住在哪裡嗎？

▶ **Has** anybody returned his books to the library yet? 有人已經還書給圖書館了嗎？

(e) 主詞被 each 或 every 修飾，或主詞為 each（代名詞）時，後接單數動詞或單數助動詞。

USAGE PRACTICE

▶ Every student in the school **wears** a badge. 這個學校的每一個學生都戴著徽章。

▶ Each child **was** given a piece of cake. 每一個小孩都得到一片蛋糕。

▶ Each girl **has** her own duty to perform. 每一個女孩都有自己要盡的義務。

▶ Every boy and girl **was** given a warm welcome. 每一個男孩和女孩都受到溫暖的歡迎。

▶ Each tin on the shelf **contains** cookies. 架上的每一個罐子裡都有餅乾。

▶ Each of the girls **has** cleaned her own room. 每一個女孩都已把自己的房間清理乾淨。

▶ Each of us **has** been tested. 我們每一個都被測試過了。

▶ Each of the boys **has** a dollar. 每一個男生都有一元。

(f) none of、much (of) 或 many a 接不可數名詞或單數可數名詞作主詞時，要用單數動詞或單數助動詞。

USAGE PRACTICE

▶ None of this business **concerns** me. 這件事跟我一點關係都沒有。

▶ Much of the ink **was** spilt on the floor. 很多的墨水灑在地板上。

▶ Much of the food **has** gone bad. 許多的食物都已腐壞了。

▶ Much of their property **was** lost in the fire. 他們大半的財產已付之一炬。

▶ Much work **has** been done within the last few days. 近幾天內完成了許多工作。

▶ There **has** not been much trouble over this matter. 這件事情不曾有過很多麻煩。

▶ Many a man **has** died for his honor. 許多人為了榮譽而捐軀。

▶ Many a book **has** been torn to pieces by her child. 許多書都被她的小孩撕成碎片。

 不定代名詞 much 作主詞時，多指「事物」，後接單數動詞或單數助動詞。

▶ Much **has** been said, but nothing has been done. 說了很多，但是一樣也沒做。

(g) 單數指示代名詞 this 和 that 作主詞時，後接單數動詞或單數助動詞。

USAGE PRACTICE

▶ This **is** the first time I have played tennis. 這是我第一次打網球。

▶ That **was** the woman I was telling you about. 那就是我之前跟你說的那個女人。

▶ That **was** the day when I fell into the river. 那就是我掉進河裡的那一天。

(h) 有些複數形態但表示單數涵義的名詞作主詞時，例如學科名稱 (mathematics、linguistics、economics) 等，要用單數動詞或單數助動詞。而有些字單複數同形，要視語意來判定動詞的使用。

USAGE PRACTICE

▶ There **has** been no news about it yet. 至今仍然沒有它的消息。

▶ The wages of sin **is** death. 罪惡的代價是死亡。

▶ Mathematics **is** her favorite subject. 數學是她最喜歡的學科。

▶ Economics **was** one of the subjects he took. 經濟學是他選修的科目之一。

▶ Politics **is** an uncertain world. 政治是不確定的世界。

▶ *The Sunday News* **is** a weekly newspaper. 《週日新聞》是一份週報。

▶ The means **was** effective. 這方法很有效。（→單數）

▶ All possible means of escape **have** been attempted.
所有可能逃脫的方法都嘗試過了。（→複數）

 有時候，上述這類名詞表示其他意思時，會被歸類為複數名詞，後接複數動詞或複數助動詞。

▶ His politics **are** rather radical. 他的政治理念相當激進。

▶ Even after her husband's death, her means **were** ample.
即使在她的丈夫過世後，她的收入還是很足夠。

(i) 當兩個名詞合指同一個人或事物時，後接單數動詞。

USAGE PRACTICE

▶ Bread and butter **was** his only food. 奶油麵包是他僅有的食物。

▶ My friend and adviser **has** come. 我的朋友兼顧問已經來了。

(j) 表示「金額、距離、時間、重量、長度」的複數名詞被視為一個整體，後接單數動詞。

基礎文法寶典❹
Essential English Usage & Grammar

▶ Don't you think that $50,000 **is** a large sum? 你不認為五萬元是一筆大數目嗎？

▶ Ten kilometers **is** quite a distance to walk. 十公里是一段相當遠的步行距離。

▶ Three meters **is** about ten feet. 三公尺大約等於十英尺。

17-2 複數主詞接複數動詞的情況

	be 動詞	助動詞 do	助動詞 have	一般動詞現在式
第一人稱 (we)、第二人稱 (you)、第三人稱 (they, the boys...)	are/were	do/did	have/had	原形

(a) 主詞為複數（包括所有的人稱）時，要用複數動詞或複數助動詞。

▶ We **are** going out now. 我們現在正要外出。

▶ We **are** not interested in the project. 我們對這個計畫不感興趣。

▶ How long **have** you been waiting? 你們已經等了多久？

▶ They **come** and **go** as they **like**. 他們隨自己喜歡來去自如。

▶ They **were** in the kitchen when he came. 當他來的時候，他們在廚房裡。

▶ **Do** they know the way? 他們知道路嗎？

▶ All the flowers **are** in the vase. 所有的花都在花瓶裡。

▶ Our neighbors **were** annoyed when we turned on the radio loudly.
  當我們把收音機開得很大聲時，我們的鄰居們很生氣。

▶ The rooms **have** not been tidied up yet. 這些房間還沒有整理好。

▶ The birds **have** all flown away. 鳥兒們全都飛走了。

(b) 複數指示代名詞 these 和 those 作主詞時，後接複數動詞或複數助動詞。

▶ These **are** the girls who **have** offered to help us. 這些就是提議要幫我們的女孩子們。

▶ These **are** the books I want you to read. 這些是我想要你去讀的書。

▶ Those **are** the people who **are** organizing the fair. 那些就是籌備商品展售會的人。

(c) a few、few、several、various、both、many 等字或大於一的數字皆用來修飾複數可數名詞，要用複數動詞或是複數助動詞。

USAGE PRACTICE

▶ A few parents **are** angry. 一些父母很生氣。

▶ A few seeds **were** planted in the pot. 在盆子裡播些種子。

▶ Few men **are** able to do it better than he. 很少人能做得比他更好。

▶ Several news items **have** been cut from this page. 這頁有好幾則新聞報導已被刪掉。

▶ Several women **are** working in the field. 幾位婦女正在田裡工作。

▶ Various people **have** agreed to support my proposal. 許多人已經同意支持我的提議。

▶ Both rulers **are** broken. 兩把尺都壞了。

▶ Both boys **are** wearing swimming trunks. 兩個男孩都穿著泳褲。

▶ Both this book and that one **are** good. 這本書和那本書都很好。

▶ Both the men **have** applied for a work permit. 這兩個男子都已經申請工作許可證。

▶ Many errors **have** been discovered in his work. 在他的作品中已被發現許多錯誤。

▶ Many insects **do** not fly. 許多昆蟲不會飛。

▶ There **were** three boys in the room. 房間裡有三個男孩。

 不定數量代名詞 both 或 many 等作主詞時，也要用複數動詞。

▶ Both of us **want** to watch the procession. 我們兩個人都想要看遊行。

▶ Many of the mangoes **are** overripe. 這些芒果中有許多都太熟了。

(d) 有些單數形態但表示複數涵義的名詞作主詞時（如 people、police、public、cattle 等），要用複數動詞或複數助動詞。

USAGE PRACTICE

▶ Twelve dozen **cost** twenty dollars. 十二打索價二十元。

▶ About 450 million people **live** in the country. 那國家約有四億五千萬人。

▶ The public have been asked to help generously. 民眾已被要求要全力協助。

基礎文法寶典 ❹
Essential English Usage & Grammar

▶ The police are tracking down the escaped convict. 警察正在追蹤逃犯。

(e) 兩個以 and 連接的單數名詞指不同的人、事、物時，要用複數動詞或複數助動詞。

▶ My father and mother **are** not at home. 我的父母不在家。

▶ Fire and water **do** not agree. 水火不相容。

(f) 「the + 形容詞」構成表全體的詞（如 the young、the poor、the hungry），要用複數動詞或複數助動詞。

▶ The young **feel** that freedom is very important. 年輕人認為自由很重要。

▶ The poor **are** usually found in slum areas. 窮人通常待在貧民窟裡。

小練習

請在空格中填入正確的 be 動詞 is、are 或 am。

1. The gates of his house _____ painted blue.

2. What _____ you doing this evening?

3. They _____ having roast chicken for dinner tonight.

4. You _____ happy with the results of the competition, _____ you?

5. The oranges _____ ripe already. _____（否定）the gardener going to pick them?

6. Where _____ the feather duster? The table _____ full of dust.

7. The streets _____ very crowded today because it _____ a public holiday.

8. He _____ willing to drive you home if you _____ leaving now.

9. She _____ always unaware of the things happening around her.

10. The prices of fish and meat _____ rising steadily these days.

11. I _____ ready to leave. _____ they here yet?

12. Some plates _____ missing from the dinner set.

13. One of the girls _____ waiting for you outside.

14. Where _____ the rest of the class? We _____ supposed to go to the hall in ten minutes.

15. He _____ better at athletics than I _____ .

16. The airport here _____ never flooded, even when there _____ a heavy downpour.

17. It _____ not very pleasant to live in the heart of the city. There _____ a lot of noise around.

18. Many of the immigrants _____ successful merchants. Some _____ on the police force, and others _____ to be found in the legal and medical professions.

☞ 更多相關習題請見本章應用練習 Part 1～Part 8。

17-3 必須注意的特殊情況

(a) 必須判斷真正的主詞或先行詞是單數或複數。

> **USAGE PRACTICE**
>
> ▶ The quality of bananas **was** not good. 香蕉的品質不好。
>
> ▶ The conditions of work **are** not desirable. 工作的環境不甚理想
>
> ▶ The condition of the rooms **is** not healthy. 這些房間的狀況不利健康。
>
> ▶ One of the boys **wants** to see you. 這些男孩中有一個想要見你。
>
> ▶ He is one of the actors who **are** highly paid. 他是待遇高的演員們之一。
>
> ▶ He is the only one of the actors who **is** highly paid. 他是這些演員中唯一待遇高的一位。
>
> ▶ This is one of the books that **were** torn that day. 這是那天被撕破的書之一。
>
> ▶ This is the only one of the books that **was** torn. 這是那些書中唯一被撕破的一本。

(b) 主詞是集合名詞時，如果指的是「一群人或物的整體」，要用單數動詞或單數助動詞。

> **USAGE PRACTICE**
>
> ▶ There **was** a big crowd at the stadium yesterday. 昨天球場裡有一大群人。
>
> ▶ Our team **has** done very well. 我們的隊表現得很好。
>
> ▶ Our team **is** going to play against that team tomorrow. 本隊明天將要和那一隊比賽。
>
> ▶ Our community **is** small. 我們的社區很小。
>
> ▶ The audience **was** very pleased with his performance. 觀眾非常喜歡他的表演。
>
> ▶ The committee **is** going to issue its report. 委員會將要發佈報告。
>
> ▶ The staff **has** sent a petition to the principal. 學校職員已經向校長請願。

▶ The staff **is** paid monthly. 全體職員都領月薪。

▶ The family **has** moved into a new house. 那一家人已經搬進新家。

▶ The army **was** advancing when it was attacked from behind.

這軍隊後方遭攻擊時,正在向前進擊。

▶ The board **is** holding a meeting now. 委員會現在正開會。

(c) 主詞是集合名詞時,如果指的是「團體中的所有個體成員」,要用複數動詞或複數助動詞。

▶ The committee **have** not given their consent to the proposal. 委員們還沒有同意這個提議。

▶ The group **have** all won badges for their school. 組員們全都為他們的學校贏得獎章。

▶ The audience **are** clapping their hands loudly. 觀眾們正在大聲鼓掌。

▶ The staff themselves **are** not pleased with their working conditions.

這些職員本身不滿意他們的工作環境。

▶ The family **are** fond of swimming. 這家人都喜歡游泳。

▶ The team **are** going to bring their own rackets. 隊員們將要帶自己的球拍。

(d) either...or 或 neither...nor 連接兩個主詞時,動詞與最接近的主詞一致。

▶ Either you or she **is** mistaken. 不是你就是她弄錯了。

▶ Neither you nor I **am** wrong. 你沒有錯,我也沒有錯。

▶ Neither she nor I **have explained** it. 她或我都還沒有解釋這件事。

▶ Neither this dress nor those two **are** suitable. 這件洋裝或另外那兩件洋裝都不適合。

▶ **Neither** these three **nor** that one **is** up to standard. 這三個或那一個都沒有達到標準。

(e) 「數量詞 + of + 名詞/代名詞」作主詞時,動詞要與名詞/代名詞一致。

▶ **Have** any of you had lunch yet? 你們當中有人吃過午餐了嗎?

▶ Most of it **has** been eaten. 大部份已經被吃掉了。

▶ Most of the dresses **have** been sold. 大部份的洋裝已經賣出了。

▶ Most of the water **is** dirty. 大部分的水很髒。

▶ Most of the girls **are** in the room already. 大部分的女孩已經在房間裡了。

▶ Some of the paint **has** been used to paint the door. 一些油漆已被用來漆這扇門。

▶ Some of the boys **are** taking part in the race. 一些男孩正在參加賽跑。

▶ Some of the food **has** been left on the table. 一些食物留在餐桌上。

▶ A lot of the students **are** not pleased with the idea. 許多學生不喜歡這個主意。

▶ A lot of the money **was** used to help the poor. 很多錢被用來幫助窮人。

▶ Almost two-thirds of the oranges **were** bad. 幾乎有三分之二的柳橙壞了。

▶ About two-thirds of the sugar **was** spilt. 約有三分之二的砂糖灑了出來。

▶ Three-quarters of the marbles **are** mine. 四分之三的彈珠是我的。

▶ Three-quarters of the land **belongs** to him. 四分之三的土地屬於他的。

(f) all 可以修飾可數或不可數名詞。修飾複數可數名詞時，要用複數動詞；修飾不可
數名詞時，要用單數動詞。

USAGE PRACTICE

▶ All the food **has** been eaten. 所有的食物都已吃完了。

▶ All the information on this topic **has** been sent out. 有關這個主題的所有資訊都已寄出。

▶ All the ice cream **has** been bought by him. 所有的冰淇淋都被他買走了。

▶ All the money in the safe **belongs** to my parents. 保險箱裡所有的錢都是我父母的。

▶ All his work **has** been wasted. 他所有的努力都白費了。

▶ All the boys **have** gone home. 所有的男孩都已經回家了。

▶ All scouts **are** to report for duty at eight o'clock. 所有的童子軍都要在八點報到準備值勤。

 all 當代名詞時，如果是指「每件事物」，要用單數動詞；如果是指「所有的人」，要用複數動詞。

▶ All **is** well. 一切都很好。(每件事物)
▶ All **has** been done. 一切都已經做好了。(每件事物)
▶ All of them **want** to join the game. 他們全部都想參加比賽。(所有的人)
▶ All **are** eager to start on the trip. 所有人都渴望動身旅行。(所有的人)
▶ The girls are not here. All **have** gone home. 女孩們不在這裡。她們全部都回家了。(所有的人)

(g) 含有 with、as well as 或 like 引導的插入句時，動詞仍須與前面的主詞一致。

小練習

請在空格中填入正確的 be 動詞 is 或 are。

1. Our badminton team _____ to compete in the tournament, but the team _____ expected to provide their own transportation there.

2. The school choir _____ going to take part in the contest.

3. The crowd _____ throwing stones at the police.

4. The group themselves _____ too busy with their work at the present.

5. Crime _____ to be eliminated at all costs. Great pains _____ taken by lawful authorities to cut down the crime rate that _____ rising.

6. A swarm of bees _____ attacking the boys. _____ （否定） anyone going to do anything about it?

7. The bouquet of flowers which you _____ going to present to the visitor _____ in the living room.

8. The crew _____ doing their best to keep the ship from crashing into the iceberg.

9. A few pieces from that set of china _____ broken.

10. The audience _____ showing their anger at the prolonged delay in the program.

11. The band which _____ going to accompany the singer tonight _____ a well-known group from Willington.

12. The troupe of dancers that _____ performing at the nightclub tonight _____ from Spain.

13. Much of his money _____ wasted on such projects. It _____ uncertain how much he actually loses.

14. The committee _____ having a meeting this morning. All the members _____ expected to be present.

15. There _____ no other means of transportation except by boat; but even then, the journey _____ quite risky.

16. None of the bananas _____ ripe. You can take either the oranges or the apples that _____ in the refrigerator instead.

17. Some of the bananas in the basket _____ unripe.

18. The only means of getting those goods _____ through that man in the shop.

☞ 更多相關習題請見本章應用練習 Part 9～Part 12。

17-4 主詞與代名詞的一致性

(a) 代名詞與其所指涉的名詞在格、性、數上必須一致。

USAGE PRACTICE

▶ The girl looked at **herself** in the mirror. **She** was surprised at **her** own transformation.
女孩看著鏡子中的自己，她對自己的轉變感到驚訝。

(b) 有時將無生命的物體或抽象名詞擬人化，可以使用人稱代名詞。

USAGE PRACTICE

▶ The warship has lost all **his** glory. 這艘軍艦已經失去所有的光彩。

▶ Fortune has **her** whims and fancies. 命運充滿幻想和想像。

(c) 對於不確定性別的人物，傳統上一律使用代名詞 he。

USAGE PRACTICE

▶ A teacher has to prepare **his** lessons before **he** teaches **his** class. 上課前，老師必須備課。

Chapter 17 　應用練習

PART 1

請在空格中填入正確的 be 動詞 is 或 are。

基礎文法寶典❹
Essential English Usage & Grammar

1. All these instruments _____ new; so _____ the box and the leather case.

2. Where _____ the vegetables? Where _____ the salt? No, the soup _____ not ready yet.

3. The engine of the car _____ not running. Do you know what _____ wrong with it?

4. His continued absence from school _____ causing some concern to his teachers. One of them _____ going to his house tonight.

5. The blade in the razor _____ rusty. _____ there any new blades in the drawer?

6. The lights in the hall _____ not on yet, but the one in my room _____.

7. I do not think that any one of us _____ capable of doing this.

8. They do these things so quietly that nobody _____ ever sure of what _____ actually happening.

9. There _____ a common saying that no news _____ good news.

10. The writer and poet _____ dead, but his works _____ still very popular.

11. The rise and fall of the tide _____ due to the influence of the moon.

12. You _____ to blame, or else he _____.

13. Every day, Mary travels twenty kilometers which _____ quite a long distance. This _____ why she looks so tired when she turns up for work at the office.

14. Every little boy and girl _____ given a present by the priest who _____ dressed up as Santa Claus.

15. The standard of English in that school _____ very high. That _____ why a large number of students there get good grades in the English exam every year.

16. There _____ ten decimeters in a meter.

17. A hundred and thirty kilometers an hour _____ a speed no traffic policeman will allow.

18. Gold and diamonds _____ much sought-after.

PART 2

請在空格中填入正確的 be 動詞 is 或 are。

1. A crowd of people _____ moving toward the market. _____ something happening there?

2. The scenery from the top of the hill _____ breathtaking.

3. Dust _____ stirred up when cars pass along this road.

4. Herds of elephants _____ often seen around these areas.

5. The price of tomatoes _____ lower in the villages than in the towns.

6. The luggage _____ placed in a separate car.

7. A number of students in this class _____ over fifteen years old.

8. There _____ not much entertainment in that small town, and the streets _____ usually empty by ten p.m.

9. That stack of newspapers _____ to be thrown away or burnt.

10. Some scenes in the play _____ very exciting, but some lack zest.

11. The results of the examination _____ quite disappointing this year.

12. There _____ rumors that the treasure _____ hidden in these parts of the island.

13. The family _____ not on speaking terms with each other after the quarrel.

14. There _____ crowds of people along the road waiting to see the procession.

15. Civics lessons _____ given once a week by the school principal himself.

16. The rate of population growth _____ increasing alarmingly, and the government _____ doing all it can to control it.

17. Water _____ stored in those reservoirs. It _____ purified and supplied through pipes to the houses.

18. There _____（否定）anything you can do now. Every one of us _____ affected by the new program.

19. Each man _____ carrying a briefcase and an umbrella. Some of the men _____ walking toward the cars now.

20. Tokyo, which _____ the largest city in the world, _____ also the capital of Japan.

PART 3

請在空格中填入正確的 be 動詞 is 或 are。

1. _____ there enough cakes for all the guests?

2. Which of these dresses _____ the most suitable one?

3. Only a little space _____ needed for the cupboard.

4. Every person _____ to leave the room except the one who _____ going to help me clean up.

5. None of the girls are writing on that topic, which _____ quite a difficult one.

6. Both men _____ willing to take on the job, and both of them _____ equally capable.

7. All parts of the building _____ surrounded by the police, who _____ out to catch the thief.

8. That part of the chicken _____ reserved for Uncle Thomas, who _____ very fond of it.

9. There _____ plenty of potatoes in the sack, but there _____ only a little milk in the bottle.

10. "_____ there any food left for me?" "Yes, there _____ a lot left."

11. Which part in the play _____ she trying out for? I don't think she _____ a very good actress.

12. The idea of being stranded on a desert island _____ appealing to us at all.

13. A cup of tea _____ very refreshing when you _____ tired and thirsty.

14. How much time _____ there before the game starts? All of us _____ waiting impatiently.

15. A little bit of flour _____ enough for this dish. The other ingredients listed here _____ not necessary.

16. His knowledge of the subject _____ extensive but more research _____ necessary if he is to prove his point.

17. Fish and chips _____ what every boarder here eats for breakfast.

18. The police _____ hot on the tracks of the thieves.

19. No news _____ good news though I must add that anxiety _____ present all the same.

20. Your fears _____ groundless as success _____ certain to be in your hands soon.

PART 4

請在空格中填入正確的 is、are、has 或 have。

1. Both of them _____ been to the party.

2. All the flour _____ been used to make the cakes.

3. _____ any of you got a penknife? The one I have _____ too blunt.

4. It _____ a pity that so many people _____ bored.

5. Their advice _____ been taken, but no good _____ come out of it.

6. David and a few of his friends _____ playing in the playground. Each of them _____ a toy and one of them _____ brought a basket of food, too.

7. A number of people _____ come to him for help; but his time and money _____ limited, and he can't do much.

8. Rice _____ the staple food of Asians. Almost every Asian family _____ rice for lunch and dinner every day.

9. Their shouting _____ very loud. Tell them that they _____ not to make so much noise.

10. All _____ confused by what _____ happening, and none of them _____ eager to explain.

11. Most of the members of the committee _____ agreed on this and _____ decided to drop the matter.

12. All this equipment _____ old-fashioned and unsuitable.

13. None of the boys _____ here when I need help. At other times, there _____ so many of them around.

14. "_____ there any cookies left?" "Yes, I think there _____ a can of them in the cupboard."

15. No news of them _____ arrived yet. All I have learnt so far _____ that they _____ gone into hiding from the soldiers who _____ hunting for them.

16. Work comes first and both of you _____ to complete it before anything else _____ done.

17. A group of tourists _____ tired after having walked five kilometers, which _____ quite a distance. The heat _____ not helped to make their tour more enjoyable.

18. This _____ one of the best movies that _____ been produced so far. It _____ the only one that _____ won so many awards at the film festival.

19. It appears that no one _____ at home. Where _____ everybody gone?

PART 5

請在空格中填入正確的 was、were、do、does、has 或 have。

1. The workers _____ not told what to do about the decoration of the house.

2. The bus _____ here a moment ago, but it _____ left.

3. They usually _____ their dinner at seven o'clock. _____ visit them before eight o'clock.

4. _____ she returned your tape recorder to you? When she _____ , will you lend it to me?

5. There _____ an exhibition of batik paintings at the Art Gallery last month. _____ you ever been there?

6. "What _____ she _____ in the house every day?" "Oh, she _____ a baby to care for."

7. A suspicious-looking character _____ standing by the bridge just now. I _____ see him there now.

8. A wolf _____ killed several lambs in the village, but no one _____ been able to capture it yet.

9. _____ he lost his voice? He _____ seem to be making himself heard.

10. The money _____ invested in shares.

11. Every town in this state _____ linked by the railroad.

12. All the boys in his family _____ athletic.

13. Both machines _____ in working condition.

14. Nobody _____ interested in knowing where they had gone.

15. Everything _____ arranged, _____ （否定） it?

16. All the windows in the house _____ broken.

17. All the men _____ in the fields. Nobody _____ in the house.

18. Nearly every seat on the bus _____ occupied. There _____ not enough room for all of us.

19. All of us _____ willing to stand by you; we _____ not afraid of his threats.

20. Neither of the rooms _____ very big, but they _____ cool and airy.

21. There _____ many things to be done, yet there _____ plenty of time to do them.

22. There _____ no one else living in that house except the old gentleman.

PART 6

請依提示在空格中填入正確的現在簡單式動詞。

1. Economics _____ (*be*) an interesting subject.

2. One of the players _____ (*be*) not feeling well.

3. He _____ (*be*) one of the speakers who _____ (*be*) always chosen to take part in debates.

4. The population _____ (*be*) small, but there _____ (*be*) no doubt that the nation's economy _____ (*be*) improving.

5. He _____ (*be*) the only member of his family who _____ (*respect*) the wishes of his parents.

6. None _____ (*be*) so understanding as those who _____ (*have*) experienced the same trouble.

7. Though the weather _____ (*be*) cloudy and cold, a party of merrymakers _____ (*be*) out to enjoy themselves. They _____ (*have*) brought a picnic basket that _____ (*be*) stuffed with food and drinks.

8. Mathematics _____ (*be*) an important subject in school. Every student, boy or girl, _____ (*be*) encouraged to do well in it.

9. The sand along the beaches _____ (*be*) white and fine. When high tide _____ (*come*), it _____ (*wash*) up unwanted materials and seaweeds which _____ (*be*) then left on the white sand.

10. Honesty _____ (*be*) the best policy, but some people _____ (*think*) that there _____ (*be*) times when honesty _____ (*fail*) to be rewarding.

11. Traffic _____ (*be*) heavy along the highway. A series of accidents _____ (*occur*) there especially when the weather _____ (*be*) bad and the roads _____ (*be*) slippery.

12. Billiards _____ (*be*) his favorite game. His interest in the game _____ (*keep*) him in the billiard room for hours.

13. The price of apples _____ (*be*) rising steadily at the market. I think the retailers _____ (*be*) responsible for the rise.

14. When one of the teachers _____ (*be*) absent, another _____ (*replace*) her until she _____ (*come*) back.

15. Tin and rubber _____ (*have*) risen in price.

16. A good man and respected citizen _____ (*have*) passed away.

17. Many a person _____ (*do*) not know whether he _____ (*be*) doing right or wrong sometimes.

PART 7

請在提示中選擇正確的形式填入空格中。

1. Lightning _____ (*flash, flashes*) across the dark sky, and a loud clap of thunder _____ (*is, are*) heard.

2. Everyone _____ (*has, have*) gone to sleep. All the lights _____ (*is, are*) off now.

3. Our holiday _____ (*last, lasts*) for seven weeks, and this time all of us _____ (*are, is*) going to Rainbow Valley.

4. Some members of the club _____ (*want, wants*) to organize a contest to raise funds.

5. The professor _____ (*know, knows*) a lot of people. His time _____ (*is, are*) always occupied in contact with people.

6. People in every city _____ (*is, are*) much the same, and there _____ (*is, are*) not much difference in this one.

7. His success overnight _____ (*has, have*) turned his head, for he _____ (*think, thinks*) his past years of poverty _____ (*is, are*) over.

8. Everything that she _____ (*do, does*) _____ (*seem, seems*) to be wrong.

9. Loads of sand _____ (*was, were*) dumped by the roadside so that there _____ (*was, were*) hardly any space for cars to pass.

10. The color of the patterns _____ (*do, does*) not suit me, but the patterns themselves _____ (*is, are*) all right.

11. Exercise _____ (*keep, keeps*) your body fit and _____ (*give, gives*) you a fresh, healthy look.

12. As the colony of ants _____ (*approach, approaches*), a deathly silence _____ (*seem, seems*) to envelop the whole area.

13. Neither of the cars _____ (*go, goes*) very fast, but their durability _____ (*is, are*) amazing.

14. This set of books _____ (*cost, costs*) over a hundred dollars, but they _____ (*are, is*) worth it.

15. The news on the radio _____ (*say, says*) that the price of coffee _____ (*is, are*) falling rapidly.

16. The money _____ (*has, have*) been stolen, and so _____ (*has, have*) all the silver plates.

一致性
Chapter 17

17. Much time _____ (*has, have*) been wasted; not one of the boys _____ (*has, have*) done any work.

18. Chicken _____ (*be*) more tender than turkey.

19. These plants _____ (*grow*) well in marshy lands because they _____ (*need*) plenty of water. There _____ (*be*) another variety which _____ (*survive*) only in well-drained land.

20. The boxes _____ (*be*) loaded onto the truck, which _____ (*deliver*) them to the shops.

PART 8

請依提示在空格中填入正確的現在簡單式動詞。

1. Much of what he _____ (*say*) _____ (*be*) nonsense. That _____ (*be*) why no one ever _____ (*listen*) to him.

2. Billions of dollars _____ (*have*) been spent on space projects. To some, man's landing on the moon _____ (*be*) a worthwhile investment. Others _____ (*feel*) that the money _____ (*be*) wasted.

3. The transport of dairy products _____ (*be*) undertaken by the government. The government _____ (*provide*) trucks which _____ (*carry*) the products to the cities.

4. Mumps _____ (*be*) an infectious disease and children or adults _____ (*catch*) it quickly from another.

5. Linguistics _____ (*be*) a most interesting subject. Being able to analyze languages _____ (*be*) a wonderful accomplishment.

6. A bunch of bananas _____ (*be*) cheap, but oranges and grapes _____ (*be*) not.

7. A dozen pencils _____ (*cost*) a dollar, but a box of crayons _____ (*cost*) more.

8. Half the class _____ (*have*) gone for home science lessons and the other half _____ (*have*) gone for sewing lessons.

9. Her condition _____ (*be*) not serious now. Rest and quiet _____ (*be*) all she _____ (*need*) to get better.

10. None of the girls _____ (*like*) to talk to that newcomer. Her conceit and overbearing manner _____ (*be*) more than they can bear.

11. Did you know that an adult human _____ (*breathe*) in and out about 25, 000 times a day?

Breathing _____ (*draw*) air into the lungs, part of which _____ (*diffuse*) through the walls of the lungs and _____ (*reach*) the blood in the lung capillaries.

12. Now, it _____ (*be*) raining heavily, and there _____ (*be*) nothing we can do.

13. Honey _____ (*be*) obtained from bees. The bees _____ (*collect*) nectar from the flowers and this _____ (*be*) turned into honey.

14. The nearness of the sandy beach _____ (*enable*) many local people to reach it by car.

15. It _____ (*be*) a fine morning today. There _____ (*be*) not a cloud in the sky.

16. The menu for lunch and dinner _____ (*vary*) according to the day of the week.

17. No one _____ (*listen*) to him because what he _____ (*say*) _____ (*do*) not make any sense.

18. Wisdom _____ (*be*) not obtained from mere studying. Experience _____ (*count*) a great deal.

19. Here _____ (*come*) someone I _____ (*want*) you to meet.

20. The captain of the guards _____ (*have*) orders to shoot any intruder in the camp.

PART 9

請在空格中填入正確的 be 動詞 is 或 are。

1. The judges of the babies' contest _____ divided in their opinions.

2. That girl, as well as her brother, _____ very mischievous.

3. Neither the king nor his ministers _____ in favor of war.

4. A few plants have been damaged by the storm. It is fortunate that most of the seedlings _____ covered by coconut leaves.

5. The ship, with its crew and passengers, _____ believed to be lost at sea.

6. Two-thirds of the estate _____ left to his youngest son. The remaining part _____ to be shared among the rest of the family.

7. Four parts of the field _____ planted with corn. The rest _____ left to lie fallow.

8. Our shop, with all its contents, _____ insured for 50,000 dollars which _____ quite a large sum.

9. I heard that the coach, as well as the players, _____ traveling to the city.

10. The girl, like her brothers, _____ active in sports.

11. The problems of governing a country _____ wide and varied.

12. His knowledge of the Chinese vernaculars _____ extensive and deep.

13. The rise in the price of raw materials _____ due chiefly to the increased demand.

14. Lucy and Jane are sisters. Both of them, like their brother, _____ artistic.

15. The occupants of the house _____ away on holiday at the moment.

16. There _____ much of the cake left after the party was over.

17. Only one of the answers _____ right, but neither Mary nor her classmates _____ aware of that.

18. Some of the audience _____ using their binoculars to get a clearer view of the performance.

PART 10

請在空格中填入正確的 do、does、has 或 have。

1. The hands of the clock _____ not seem to have moved at all.

2. The crate of apples _____ been delivered to your house.

3. Each of you _____ a part in the play. All of you _____ to attend a rehearsal tomorrow.

4. Some of the children _____ not like to play on the seesaw. Their father _____ constructed some swings in the garden for them.

5. The gates of the house _____ been painted white.

6. Many of them _____ not know the truth about this incident.

7. All possible means of recovering the jewels _____ been tried.

8. Great pains _____ been taken to decorate the hall.

9. They have cleared a lot of jungle that _____ been obstructing the building of roads.

10. Some of the money _____ been returned to the owner, but the rest _____ still not been found.

11. The room is so untidy. Either the cats or the dog _____ been here.

12. Either those boys or she _____ left the gate open. Most of the goats _____ wandered out.

13. The ship, with its crew, _____ gone aground.

14. The introduction of potatoes _____ been beneficial to the country.

15. The state of his affairs _____ caused much anxiety among his close friends.

16. The suitcase, with all the bottles of drugs that it contains, _____ been confiscated by the Customs officials.

17. _____ all the members of the family live in the same house?

18. Every family in this neighborhood _____ a car.

19. _____ this book and that one give the same information, or _____ they differ?

20. None of them _____ this sort of thing unless they are in trouble.

PART 11

請依提示在空格中填入正確的現在簡單式動詞。

1. Most of the water in the villages _____ (be) obtained from wells.

2. Neither she nor I _____ (have) done the work yet.

3. Many a man _____ (have) died in trying to accomplish that feat.

4. Most of the buildings along this road _____ (be) to be pulled down.

5. Some of the members of the staff _____ (have) resigned because a few of the new terms of service _____ (be) not agreeable to them.

6. A number of students in that class _____ (be) under the age of twelve.

7. Most of the milk _____ (be) sold in either bottles or cans that _____ (have) been sterilized.

8. A lot of information about the project _____ (have) leaked out.

9. There _____ (be) still much to be done.

10. Neither these three nor that one _____ (be) suitable.

11. Each of these minerals _____ (be) found in the mountains to the north.

12. Most of the grapes _____ (be) bad. Only a few of them _____ (be) good enough to eat.

13. Neither of these two men _____ (be) very strong. Both _____ (be) suffering from a mysterious ailment.

14. No nook or corner _____ (be) to be left unexplored.

15. Neither praise nor blame _____ (seem) to have much effect on him.

16. All _____ (want) to join in the game, but none _____ (be) prepared to help me put up the poles.

17. No pains _____ (be) spared to bring kidnappers to justice.

18. A farmer's means _____ (be) decreased when there _____ (be) a reduction in the price of agricultural products.

19. The Statistics Department _____ (have) estimated that forty percent of the population of the country _____ (be) made up of young people who _____ (be) under twenty-five years of age.

20. Cooperation among the various races _____ (be) vital to the nation's prosperity.

PART 12

請依提示在空格中填入正確的現在簡單式動詞。

1. As the jury _____ (be) divided in their opinions, the court _____ (have) been adjourned to the next day.

2. All of the audience _____ (be) appreciative of the act and _____ (be) applauding for an encore.

3. The board of directors _____ (be) by no means pleased with the ways that the company _____ (be) run.

4. The economics of the project _____ (have) to be taken into account before it is launched.

5. The committee _____ (have) agreed that an increase in the annual subscription _____ (be) necessary.

6. A staff of twenty _____ (have) been chosen to see that everything runs smoothly.

7. Law and order generally _____ (prevail) after a crowd _____ (have) been dispersed by the police.

8. Two-thirds of the class _____ (be) absent because the disease has affected them, too.

9. Neither you nor she _____ (be) to participate in the festival.

10. The ocean liner, with its passengers and crew, _____ (be) tossed about by the turbulent waves that _____ (be) higher than the liner itself. All radio contact _____ (be) lost and any hope of immediate rescue _____ (be) gone.

11. The money from the estate _____ (be) to be divided among the three brothers. Two-thirds of the money _____ (go) to the eldest brother while the rest _____ (be) shared equally by the two younger brothers.

12. The boys, as well as their sister, _____ (be) going hiking. Each of them _____ (have) a backpack where all their things _____ (be) kept.

13. Many a person _____ (*have*) attempted to do the same thing but failed. Intelligence, not mere strength, _____ (*be*) the deciding factor.

14. Neither those boys nor that girl _____ (*be*) willing to go.

15. She says that neither this dress nor those two _____ (*be*) suitable. In my opinion, every one of them _____ (*be*) suitable for the occasion.

16. A troupe of Spanish dancers _____ (*have*) arrived in Cleveland and they _____ (*be*) performing in the Town Hall tonight.

17. The staff _____ (*be*) working on the first floor of the building while their office _____ (*be*) being redecorated.

PART 13

請在提示中選擇正確的形式填入空格中。

1. If each one of you _____ (*gives, give*) a dollar, we shall have more than enough money.

2. Everyone _____ (*wants, want*) to get rich as quickly as possible; so when the opportunity _____ (*comes, come*), _____ (*it, they*) _____ (*grabs, grab*) it.

3. Neither Mary nor John _____ (*is, are*) coming to the meeting. Both of them _____ (*is, are*) busy with _____ (*his, her, their*) work.

4. Each one of these boxes _____ (*contains, contain*) several thousand dollars worth of gold.

5. One of the campers _____ (*has, have*) got sick. The others _____ (*is, are*) all well.

6. There _____ (*is, are*) not much hope for their safe rescue. Everyone _____ (*is, are*) worried about them.

7. Neither your sister nor your brother _____ (*comes, come*) to this place often. The only person who _____ (*comes, come*) here regularly _____ (*is, are*) Jane.

8. "_____ (*Is, Are*) there another way to get to the place?" "Yes, there _____ (*is, are*) several other ways, but this one _____ (*is, are*) the shortest."

9. Every boy _____ (*has, have*) to bring along _____ (*his, their*) own lunch. Neither drinks nor food _____ (*is, are*) provided.

10. There _____ (*is, are*) various methods of solving this problem. Any one of them _____ (*is, are*) acceptable, but the shortest method _____ (*is, are*) the easiest one.

11. Either the girl or the boys _____ (*has, have*) been here. I know because all our food _____ (*is, are*) gone, and all the plates _____ (*is, are*) unwashed.

12. Each and every one of you _____ (*is, are*) to be here at ten o'clock. If any one of you _____ (*comes, come*) late, _____ (*he, they*) will be punished.

13. There _____ (*was, were*) lots of food; but after the party, all of _____ (*it, them*) _____ (*was, were*) gone. Each one of the boys took home some food in _____ (*his, their*) bag.

14. Not one of us _____ (*is, are*) able to sing well, so we _____ (*passes, pass*) the time by telling each other stories. Each _____ (*tells, tell*) his or her own favorite story while the others _____ (*listens, listen*).

15. All the children _____ (*has, have*) gone home with _____ (*its, her, their*) parents.

16. The information he gave us _____ (*is, are*) quite untrue. I wonder where he got _____ (*it, them*).

17. The police _____ (*has, have*) been working hard to capture that gangster, and finally _____ (*it, they*) _____ (*has, have*) succeeded.

18. Please tell the crew that _____ (*it, they*) can come on board now and that _____ (*it, they*) can start work at once.

19. The food _____ (*has, have*) already gone bad; we shall have to throw _____ (*it, them*) away.

20. Below _____ (*is, are*) a list of words. This list _____ (*gives, give*) the antonyms of certain words.

基礎文法寶典❹
Essential English Usage & Grammar

習題解答

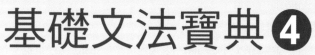

Chapter 13 解答

13-2 小練習

1. is 2. are 3. is 4. was 5. was 6. were 7. will be 8. Are/Were 9. am 10. were
11. am 12. was 13. are 14. were; were 15. were; are; Is

13-3 小練習

1. has 2. has 3. had 4. have 5. was having 6. has 7. had 8. have 9. has 10. has
11. has 12. are having 13. has 14. has 15. had 16. have 17. have 18. are having 19. had
20. Have; have

13-4 小練習

1. did 2. do/don't 3. do 4. don't 5. do 6. doesn't 7. do; don't
8. does/did; doesn't/didn't 9. Do; do 10. did 11. Does; does 12. do/don't; do 13. didn't; did
14. does/did; do; didn't

13-5 小練習

1. should; should 2. should 3. shall 4. shall 5. shall 6. should 7. shall 8. should
9. should; should 10. should 11. should 12. shall 13. shall; shall

13-6 小練習

1. would 2. would 3. Will/Would 4. will 5. will/would 6. will 7. would 8. would
9. Will/Would; will 10. would 11. would 12. will 13. will; will 14. would; would

13-7 小練習

1. could 2. could 3. can 4. can't 5. couldn't 6. can't; can 7. can 8. can 9. could
10. couldn't 11. can 12. Can; can't 13. could 14. can

13-8 小練習

1. may 2. may 3. might 4. May; may 5. might 6. might 7. might 8. may; may
9. might 10. may 11. may 12. may/might; May 13. might 14. may/might

13-9 小練習

1. had to 2. must 3. must 4. must 5. had; to 6. will have to 7. will have to 8. had; to
9. must; will have to 10. must; must 11. will have to 12. had to 13. must 14. had; to

13-10 小練習

1. The gardener ought to have burned the rubbish this morning. 2. You ought not to have driven so fast last night. 3. She ought to have taken an umbrella along just now. 4. He ought to have followed

the instructions two days ago.　5. The farmers ought to have bought modern machinery with their government loans last year.　6. It's going to rain. You ought not to have put the clothes out to dry just now.　7. The chicken coop ought to have been washed early this morning.　8. He ought not to have broken that promise last week.　9. The student ought to have been punished for the theft immediately. 10. The match ought to have started at five o'clock.　11. They ought to have cut down the tree a month ago.　12. He ought to have written to his uncle last Friday.　13. You ought not to have been so careless yesterday.　14. She ought to have left them alone last night.

13–11 小練習

1. mustn't　2. mustn't　3. needn't　4. mustn't　5. mustn't　6. needn't　7. mustn't
8. mustn't　9. needn't　10. needn't　11. needn't　12. mustn't　13. mustn't　14. needn't
15. needn't　16. mustn't

13–12 小練習

1. used to　2. used to　3. Dare　4. used to　5. used to　6. dare　7. ought not to　8. used to
9. used to　10. ought to　11. dare　12. ought to　13. dare　14. ought to; dare　15. used to; ought to

應用練習

PART 1

1. is　2. is　3. is　4. is　5. are　6. are　7. is　8. is　9. is　10. is　11. are　12. is　13. is
14. are　15. are　16. Are　17. are　18. is

PART 2

1. He does not have a cold now.　2. We have not taken the car to the garage.　3. John does not have a dog named "Spot."　4. The washerwoman has not brought back the sheets.　5. I have not had my haircut.　6. We do not have visitors staying with us at present.　7. I am not having difficulty completing the project. I have not handed the job over to Mr. Hanson.　8. The children did not have measles last year.　9. She had not broken her promise　10. They do not have the room cleaned daily. 11. He does not have brown eyes and black hair.　12. We did not have coffee at Jane's house just now. 13. My aunt does not often have headaches.　14. All the students have not had inoculations against cholera.　15. That hotel does not have a lot of tourists staying there.

PART 3

1. have　2. was　3. aren't; are　4. Has　5. is; have　6. has; has　7. is; has　8. have; is
9. have; had　10. is; isn't; isn't　11. Are; are　12. Weren't; are; are　13. has; have; is
14. was; had; was; had　15. isn't; was; was; had

PART 4

1. do   2. do; don't   3. does   4. Does; doesn't   5. did; didn't   6. Does; does   7. don't; do

8. Don't; do   9. doesn't; does   10. didn't   11. don't; do   12. Do; don't   13. Do; do   14. don't; did

PART 5

1. didn't   2. don't   3. doesn't; does   4. Did; done   5. did; do; Did   6. Do; don't

7. didn't; did; didn't   8. do; Do; do   9. doing   10. don't; do; Do   11. doesn't; does

12. doesn't; don't; done   13. did; didn't; did; didn't   14. don't; does; does

PART 6

1. Do they eat meat on Fridays?   2. Does that baby cry for his milk every three hours?   3. Did she miss the flight to Tokyo yesterday?   4. Does Vincent play golf every Saturday?   5. Did the children behave themselves very well yesterday?   6. Did anybody deliver the parcel to the house just now? 7. Did he do very well in his mathematics test?   8. Do the boys from next door always crawl through the hole in the fence?   9. Did the principal present him with a prize for being the best student of the year?   10. Did the taxi go through the red light?   11. Does he grumble about his work?   12. Did anyone see him being attacked?   13. Does she usually leave the house in a hurry in the morning?   14. Did they speak to the officer about the matter?   15. Do you like three cubes of sugar in your coffee?   16. Does it rain almost every afternoon?

PART 7

1. did; didn't   2. is; be; does   3. is; does   4. be; do   5. do; do; is; are   6. was; did

7. Did; do   8. Do; do; is   9. did; is   10. was   11. Do; are   12. was; did   13. was; did

14. Be; don't   15. did; did; did   16. does; do; are   17. am; don't; do   18. was; was; did

PART 8

1. Don't; don't   2. is; don't   3. are; don't   4. Do; be   5. do; are   6. were; didn't

7. doesn't; Do   8. are; aren't; Do   9. do; are; am   10. is; are   11. Do; do   12. did; did

13. Does; doesn't; didn't   14. don't; does; are   15. do; is; is   16. Don't; are   17. do; am; are

18. are; are

PART 9

1. has; is; does; has   2. is; is; have   3. has; is; have   4. does; are   5. has; does   6. have; are

7. has; is; do   8. Do; have   9. have; are; have; have   10. does; have; are   11. are; has   12. is; have

13. is; has; have   14. has; has; is   15. is; are; do; has   16. have; is; has   17. do; are; have; are

18. has; has; is; is   19. does; is; has

PART 10

1. don; has; are   2. Do; don't; am   3. is; have; are   4. has; does; has   5. have; has; are
6. has; are; have   7. are; is; are   8. has; hasn't; do   9. are; have   10. have; have; is   11. is; am;
has   12. Do; are; are

PART 11

1. He hasn't got a lot of detective novels in his room.   2. She didn't go out just now.   3. They
haven't all gone to church.   4. He doesn't have a bath every morning before he goes to school.
5. They don't need warm clothes for the winter there.   6. The teacher hasn't corrected all my essays.
7. He didn't have difficulty persuading her to go out with him.   8. I haven't forgotten to bring my
notes along.   9. They didn't submit their application forms on the last day.   10. He hasn't got enough
money to last him a lifetime.   11. She doesn't have the windows washed every week.   12. We haven't
agreed to his suggestion. He didn't explain it clearly to us last night.   13. We hadn't lost the game to the
opposing team.   14. She didn't feel a moment's pity for the helpless creature.   15. She didn't ask the
doctor about the condition of her grandfather.   16. They don't have any friends staying for dinner
tonight.

PART 12

1. should   2. would   3. should/would   4. Would   5. should   6. would   7. should
8. Should   9. should   10. should/would   11. Would; would   12. would; would   13. should; would
14. Would

PART 13

1. would; should   2. would   3. should   4. would; should   5. would; wouldn't
6. should; would   7. would; should/would   8. should; wouldn't   9. should; should
10. should; would   11. would   12. Should; would   13. wouldn't   14. should   15. would
16. should; would   17. would; should   18. wouldn't; would; should

PART 14

1. would   2. should   3. Would   4. should; would   5. would; should   6. should/would; would
7. would; should   8. should; would   9. should; would   10. Should   11. would; should
12. should/would; would   13. would; should   14. should; would   15. would; would
16. should; would   17. would; should   18. Would; should   19. should; would; should; would

PART 15

1. Would   2. should   3. Would   4. should   5. Would   6. should   7. would   8. should

9. would 10. should 11. would; should 12. should; Would 13. would 14. should

15. would; Should 16. would; should 17. should; would 18. would; should

PART 16

1. can't 2. could 3. Can 4. could 5. can 6. couldn't 7. couldn't 8. can 9. can

10. could 11. can 12. couldn't 13. can't 14. can 15. can 16. could 17. could 18. couldn't

19. can; can't 20. couldn't

PART 17

1. could 2. can 3. could 4. can; can 5. couldn't 6. could 7. couldn't 8. couldn't; can

9. can; can't 10. can; can't 11. couldn't; could 12. can't; Could 13. couldn't; could

PART 18

1. Can; Can't 2. can't 3. Could 4. can't 5. can't 6. couldn't 7. couldn't

8. Can/Could; can't 9. could 10. Can; can't 11. Can; can't 12. Could/Can; could

13. can't; Could 14. can't; can 15. couldn't; couldn't 16. can; can't 17. could; can't

18. could; couldn't

PART 19

1. Can; can't 2. Could 3. could 4. can 5. can 6. could 7. can't 8. able to

9. Could/Can; can't 10. could 11. able to 12. Could/Can 13. able to 14. can 15. Can 16. can

17. Could/Can; could 18. couldn't; could 19. couldn't

PART 20

1. may 2. might 3. May 4. may 5. may 6. may/might 7. may/might 8. may/might

9. might 10. may; may 11. May 12. May 13. might 14. might

PART 21

1. might 2. may/might 3. May; may 4. might; may 5. May

6. may/might; may not/might not 7. might 8. may/might 9. may; may 10. might 11. may

PART 22

1. May 2. might 3. might 4. might 5. may 6. might 7. may/might 8. May 9. May

10. may/might not 11. may not 12. may/might 13. may; might 14. may not; might

PART 23

1. have to 2. must 3. must 4. must 5. must 6. must 7. had to 8. must 9. must

10. must 11. must 12. must 13. had to 14. must 15. must 16. must 17. must 18. had to

19. mustn't; must

PART 24

1. They have to leave this week./They will have to leave this week.   2. She has to go on a diet as she is overweight./She will have to go on a diet as she is overweight.   3. We don't have to tell them where we are going./We won't have to tell them where we are going.   4. If you fail, you have to request a second chance./If you fail, you will have to request a second chance.   5. The bridge has to be repaired by next month./The bridge will have to be repaired by next month.   6. The ship has to sail within the week for Jamaica./The ship will have to sail within the week for Jamaica.   7. She has to clean the windows every week./She will have to clean the windows every week.   8. The players have to practice very hard for the tournament./The players will have to practice very hard for the tournament.   9. You have to teach the boys how to put on their ties./You will have to teach the boys how to put on their ties.   10. If you see him, tell him that he has to bring his documents to the office on Saturday./If you see him, tell him that he will have to bring his documents to the office on Saturday.   11. The workers have to complete the building for the shopping arcade by next year./The workers will have to complete the building for the shopping arcade by next year.   12. He doesn't have to sit for the examination this year./He won't have to sit for the examination this year.   13. She has to see a doctor at once. You have to persuade her to go./She will have to see a doctor at once. You will have to persuade her to go.   14. The fire has to be put out before it spreads to the gas station./The fire will have to be put out before it spreads to the gas station.

PART 25

1. He has to fill up the car tank with gas before he starts off.   2. You have to ring him up before he leaves the office.   3. She has to wait for the five o'clock bus if she misses this one.   4. They have to read more if they wish to improve their English.   5. Do we have to follow his instructions strictly?   6. Jim and Paul have to tell her about the mistake.   7. His wife has to run the shop when he is out.   8. Does he always have to depend on his father for financial support?   9. Everyone has to obey the rules of the college.   10. He has to pay all his debts by tomorrow.   11. Do I have to roll up the carpet?   12. Every person has to go through Customs when entering a foreign country.   13. You have to wipe the dust from the shelves. Do you always have to be told what to do?

PART 26

1. I will have to inform her immediately.   2. He had to stay up late last night to complete his work.   3. You have to practice on your violin regularly for the concert.   4. He had to report the theft of his new car to the police.   5. Aunt Agatha usually has to go to the doctor every month to check her blood pressure.   6. We will have to take the dog for treatment tomorrow.   7. They had to stop at the post

office on the way home.　8. He had to write out the answers at once.　9. You will have to tell them your address.　10. She always has to pay her rent on the first of the month.　11. They will have to change their clothes before they go out.　12. Did she have to warm the pan first?　13. He had to take his pen with him into the examination hall.　14. The workmen will have to come to repair the roof tomorrow.

PART 27

1. needn't　2. mustn't　3. needn't　4. mustn't　5. mustn't　6. mustn't　7. needn't
8. mustn't　9. needn't　10. needn't　11. needn't　12. needn't　13. needn't　14. mustn't
15. mustn't　16. needn't　17. needn't　18. needn't

PART 28

1. I needn't turn up for practice tomorrow, as I am not in the school choir.　2. The plaque needn't be unveiled by the Mayor himself.　3. The lawn needn't be mowed this week.　4. She has got much time; she needn't hurry.　5. They haven't graduated from a commercial school; they needn't do the accounts.　6. The alarm clock needn't be set to wake us up early tomorrow.　7. If the bell doesn't ring, you needn't assemble on the field.　8. He needn't clean and polish his own shoes every day.
9. They needn't send the child back as his parents will be coming to take him home.　10. You needn't show your passport to the immigration officer.　11. She needn't take both children to the fair.　12. They needn't obtain their parents'permission before going on the excursion.　13. We needn't stay to help them to clear the table.　14. None of the players are absent. We needn't postpone the match.

PART 29

1. ought to　2. Dare　3. used to　4. oughtn't to　5. used to　6. dare　7. oughtn't to
8. used to　9. ought to　10. dare; dare　11. used to　12. ought to　13. dare; ought to
14. ought to; daren't　15. used to　16. ought to; used to　17. ought to; used to; ought to　18. dare

Chapter 14　解答

應用練習

PART 1

1. steal　2. take　3. to leave; to go　4. go　5. to withdraw; to bring　6. accept　7. perform
8. to gather; to attend　9. make; eat　10. inform　11. to put; to give　12. to do　13. tremble
14. to give　15. to have　16. play　17. to do　18. to talk　19. study　20. to go; to do　21. to be put
22. to persuade; to lend　23. to dry　24. to open

150　基礎文法寶典❹
Essential English Usage & Grammar

1. clean   2. to bring   3. to go   4. sing; dance; roll   5. to go   6. tap   7. bring; to rain

8. to keep   9. drive   10. run; give   11. to talk   12. clean; take   13. to break   14. to interview

15. to start   16. to bring   17. to bring   18. to enter   19. to repair   20. to be cleaned   21. to turn

22. to be   23. To be   24. to give

PART 3

1. That story sounds to be true.   2. I was told not to leave the room.   3. Have you got anything for us to eat?   4. She hopes to be chosen to represent her school.   5. We must wait to hear the results of the contest.   6. You will have to study hard to pass the examination.   7. The first person to reach the finish line will be declared the winner.   8. Is there anything else to discuss?   9. The girl did not expect to get the job.   10. The poacher was warned not to trespass on the estate again.   11. The doctor advised Mr. Biggs not to smoke.   12. Will you promise not to lose this magazine?   13. I hope to receive the letter by tomorrow.   14. We understood what needed to be done when the time came.   15. I expect to complete writing the book by next Christmas.   16. The last person to finish had to stay behind to clean up the mess.   17. Amy was told not to go out alone in the dark.   18. She had to wait a long time to buy the tickets.   19. The boy scouts hope to reach the summit by nightfall.   20. It appears to be an impossible task.

Chapter 15 解答

15-5 小練習

1. Swimming   2. Walking   3. singing; dancing   4. playing   5. fishing   6. training

7. Looking   8. Walking   9. Painting   10. taking   11. reading   12. paying   13. Lying

14. washing   15. tumbling   16. Drilling   17. smoking   18. playing; playing

應用練習

PART 1

1. shopping   2. Working   3. fixing   4. mowing   5. playing   6. bullying; throwing

7. swimming   8. Collecting; gardening   9. Smoking   10. breaking   11. getting

12. spending; surfing   13. watching   14. breaking   15. speeding   16. quitting   17. buying

18. sharing

PART 2

1. your wanting; looking   2. studying; guessing   3. his smoking; doing   4. his nodding; yawning

5. your coming; Seeing; writing   6. Philip's losing; her telling   7. swimming; diving

8. our eating; drinking; doing   9. her borrowing; her returning   10. my learning; telling

11. your saying; Making   12. Teaching; the students' making   13. buying   14. urging; Sleeping

15. our leaving; leaving   16. doing   17. hurrying; making   18. getting; Washing; weeding; doing

PART 3

1. Working; traveling   2. spending   3. swimming; jogging   4. questioning; telling   5. telling

6. cleaning; having used; cleaning   7. learning; speaking; reading   8. caring; looking

9. bearing; getting; speaking   10. doing; rearranging; wiping   11. collecting; looking   12. going

13. working   14. following   15. waiting   16. learning   17. interrupting   18. knocking

PART 4

1. his being tricked   2. our talking   3. her brother's coming   4. their looking   5. our staying

6. his letting   7. altering; pestering   8. Your being   9. his coming   10. their leaving

11. weaving; his working   12. my criticizing; losing   13. my giving; your carrying

14. my interrupting; writing   15. our camping; our getting   16. the man's asking

17. my changing; sitting

PART 5

1. Seeing; believing   2. missing   3. interfering   4. helping   5. being told   6. bathing

7. Learning; learning   8. making   9. packing   10. saying; looking   11. putting   12. telling

13. walking; taking   14. wording   15. Arguing   16. smoking   17. sewing; colleting

18. Being chased   19. being punished; telling   20. crossing; making

PART 6

1. reading   2. to turn   3. receiving   4. Taking   5. say/saying   6. to learn   7. lending

8. wash; to use; use   9. repairing/to be repaired   10. climb/climbing   11. putting   12. beat/beating

13. to get   14. writing   15. to say   16. to write   17. building   18. to give   19. playing

20. to cross; try

PART 7

1. catching   2. pick/picking; give/giving   3. return   4. to work/working   5. cry/crying

6. smoking   7. to find   8. to report   9. drinking   10. to receive   11. to find   12. repairing

13. to give   14. complaining   15. to share   16. stealing   17. to make   18. walk/walking; to lock

PART 8

1. eating   2. Smoking; to give   3. to stop; writing   4. to get; lending

5. to say; to do; saying; doing　　6. Rising; to take; to have　　7. to learn; to swim　　8. arguing; to help

9. to write　　10. to play　　11. parting/to part; coming　　12. Having; to learn　　13. talking; to help

14. Memorizing; to study　　15. to sign　　16. exploring; to explore　　17. eating; to repair

18. to teach; to play

PART 9

1. translating　　2. stay; to finish　　3. to finish; making　　4. Going; to get　　5. hearing; to go

6. to stop; smoking; to take/taking　　7. resting; to have; to rest　　8. to watch; Watching; watching

9. to learn; to parachute; to take　　10. to rehearse; staying; to direct　　11. to ask; to use　　12. to enter

13. to rain; take　　14. Saying/To say; retiring　　15. to learn; saying　　16. To tell

17. to accuse; murdering　　18. tell; to do

PART 10

1. wondering; climbing　　2. smoking; eating/to eat　　3. trying　　4. disturbing; admiring

5. Being stung　　6. buying; reading　　7. camping; swimming　　8. leaving　　9. to know　　10. to do

11. putting　　12. to lend　　13. shifting　　14. to argue　　15. going　　18. to do/to be done

19. to tell; to solve

Chapter 16　解答

16–1 小練習

1. burning　　2. boring　　3. depressed　　4. broken　　5. spoken　　6. inspiring　　7. crying

8. playing　　9. reading　　10. frightened　　11. crawling　　12. amazing　　13. growing

14. heartbroken; burned　　15. escaped

16–3 小練習

1. standing　　2. worn　　3. coming　　4. stolen　　5. flying　　6. made　　7. talking　　8. leading

9. hunted　　10. hung　　11. handing　　12. singing　　13. sleeping　　14. watering　　15. cooked

16–4 小練習

1. Feeling　　2. injured　　3. Squatting　　4. disturbed　　5. Thinking　　6. Standing　　7. playing

8. Hearing　　9. trying　　10. Watching　　11. Frightened　　12. Managing　　13. Exhausted　　14. Climbing

15. Angered　　16. reading　　17. annoyed　　18. Astonished　　19. writing　　20. Startled　　21. Determined

16–5 小練習

1. Not having heard　　2. Having forgotten　　3. Having promised　　4. Having convinced

5. Having been punished　　6. having been assured　　7. Never having been　　8. not having recovered

9. Having sprained   10. Not having seen   11. Having; been killed   12. Not having been informed

13. Having found   14. Never having heard   15. Having learned   16. Having cleared; washed

17. Not having done; practiced   18. Having locked; shut   19. never having been

20. Having been scolded   21. having heard

應用練習

PART 1

1. rolling   2. mended   3. boiling   4. broken   5. doing   6. hidden   7. lying   8. gathering

9. perching   10. amused; amusing   11. running   12. traveling   13. experienced   14. frightened

15. screaming   16. finished

PART 2

1. Is there somebody upstairs playing the harmonica?   2. The dress trimmed with red ribbons and lace looked very attractive.   3. Tomorrow, there will be another bus taking you to school.   4. The bride had a long, lace veil worn by her mother at her wedding years ago.   5. We noticed some men digging up the road.   6. Not knowing the facts, he finds it hard to give an answer.   7. The team losing in the first half of the game pledged to do their best to win in the second half.   8. The tennis racket stolen by someone several days ago was recovered by my friend today.   9. The signboard hanging outside the shop is broken.   10. Needed urgently, the spare parts were flown in from the United States.   11. The soldiers were approaching, trying to launch a surprise attack.   12. This is the brochure giving you all the information on the district.   13. Exhausted, the boys refused to walk any further.   14. The school principal admired the painting painted by the art students.   15. He walked into the garden, whistling loudly.   16. The room cleaned at the beginning of the week was dirty again at the end of the week.   17. She looked at the trees swaying in the strong wind in the distance.   18. The three passengers injured in the accident were taken to the hospital.   19. The essay written by him won first prize in the competition.   20. Don't step on the mousetrap lying in the doorway.

PART 3

1. We watched the fishermen throwing nets into the sea.   2. The boy taking the salute in the march past is my brother.   3. She recognized the man wanted for murder by the police.   4. We found him hiding under the bed.   5. She took all the money kept in the safe.   6. She went to the dinner, thinking it would be over in two hours.   7. The police fired tear gas, hoping to frighten away the mob.   8. The car parked by the side of the road was damaged beyond repair.   9. The book bound in a hard cover belonged to my mother.   10. My brother is in the garden, trimming the hedge.   11. The purse lost

during the game has been found by one of the spectators.　12. Assisted by Mr. Lewis, we managed to complete the project.　13. My sister touched the pot, not realizing that it was hot.　14. I accidentally stepped into a hole dug for the purpose of planting a tree.　15. We walked up and down the room, trying to find a way to solve our problem.　16. The driver lost control of his car, hitting a pedestrian and smashing into a shop window.　17. Having been hurt during the rugby game, the boy was carried out by some members of the St. John's Ambulance Brigade.　18. We saw a beautiful painting placed in a big, carved frame.　19. Here is the notice telling me that I have been dismissed from the firm.

PART 4

1. The boy stood on the shore, watching the fishermen casting their nets into the sea.　2. Did you see a man with a long beard passing this way a few minutes ago?　3. The essay written by one of my classmates won first prize in the competition.　4. The child lost in the crowd cried with fright.　5. They chased away the young man, not knowing that he was their own son.　6. Exhausted at the end of the day, he had a very good night's sleep.　7. Peter got out of bed slowly, thinking that there was plenty of time for him to get ready　8. Hearing the bell of the ice-cream man, the children rushed out to stop him.　9. They were discussing an article written by a young lecturer in the newspaper.　10. He set out when it became dark, thinking that he could travel unseen at night.　11. Many people stood on the beach, watching the life guard rescue the drowning girl.　12. Trapped in the small room, he could not move at all.　13. They stared at the huge animal blocking their path.　14. Here is a booklet, giving some information of the most famous tourist attractions in the country.　15. Do you see something moving in the water?　16. She got on the bus, not realizing it was the wrong one.　17. I picked up the phone to call him, wondering whether he had reached home.

PART 5

1. He closed the door with a bang, striding angrily into the room.　2. I noticed two men lurking furtively near the jewelry shop.　3. Thinking it was the right time, he put forward his suggestions to them.　4. She decided that the torn and tattered dress could not be mended again.　5. The teacher was in the staff room, grading some exercise books.　6. Did you happen to notice a black car passing this way a few minutes ago?　7. There was a tractor leveling the ground.　8. The detective examined the room thoroughly, hoping to find some clue to the mysterious happenings.　9. Not knowing his real intention, I did as he suggested.　10. Flipping the case open, I got a very big shock.　11. Here is the page giving a description of the chief character in the book.　12. Pretending not to notice him, she walked to a side stall and stood there, looking at some magazines.

PART 6

1. There they are, listening to the band.   2. Riding to school, he saw an accident.   3. The girl deserted by her family and friends ran away to another village.   4. Running into the garden, he tripped over a brick.   5. Stunned by the blow, he slumped to the ground unconsciously.   6. He is in the garden, practicing the art of self-defense.   7. I did not hear the song played on the radio.   8. She is in the backyard, putting out the clothes to dry.   9. My friend is in London, taking a course in business administration.   10. The beggar slept on the sidewalk, having no home to go to.   11. He looked at the hysterical woman, wondering what had happened.   12. She thought of the days ahead, hoping that everything would go well for her.   13. Chased by the angry bull, he did not know what to do.   14. He has lost the book containing an informative account of life in the Pacific Islands.   15. Embarrassed by what he had said, she ran out of the room.

PART 7

1. Standing on the balcony, we could see the whole park.   2. Having been knocked down by a taxi, the old man was limping across the road.   3. Walking through the park, we saw some oak trees.   4. Stunned by the news, my father could find no words to say.   5. He tripped over the bucket containing water.   6. Disgusted by what he saw, he averted his face.   7. He saw the farmer setting fire to the barn.   8. The scuba divers found the wrecked launch covered with weeds.   9. Seeing that it was raining, Alan looked around for his raincoat.   10. Securely tied to the tree, the dog could only bark at the stranger.   11. Born and bred in the country, she was bewildered by the sights of the city.   12. Terrified by what she had seen, she hid her face in her hands.   13. My work all completed, I could get ready to go home.   14. Staged by the kindergarten children, the concert was a great success.   15. She tossed and turned in bed, thinking of the bleak future ahead.   16. Christmas being a holiday, we don't need to go to the office.   17. We crossed the mountainous border, Malcolm acting as a guide.

PART 8

1. Feeling sleepy, he went to bed.   2. Having finished our work, we were allowed to have a short break.   3. I saw the actors preparing themselves for the final scene.   4. Riding along the track, we saw an old man walking with a stick.   5. The soldiers trained by this captain were very good fighters.   6. Having washed the car, the boy wiped the windscreen.   7. I saw the lifeguard rescuing the swimmer.   8. Having been told not to leave the house, we did not do so.   9. Having been warned of the enemy's approach, the villagers set up barricades outside the village.   10. Seeing that the weather was fine, he went out for a walk.   11. Having worked at tall buildings before, the construction workers

did not feel dizzy at all.   12. The man wanted by the police escaped to another country.   13. Determined to pass his examination, he studied very hard.   14. The children do not like fish cooked that way.   15. Driving through the countryside, he saw fields of corn.   16. Being a sensitive person, she is easily hurt.   17. The woman giving away the prizes is the wife of the mayor.   18. The boys teasing the newcomer were told off roundly by the teacher.

PART 9

1. Having seen the movie before, he did not want to go.   2. The guests sitting in the big tent had a great view of the sports events.   3. Hurrying to catch a bus, Terry tripped over a log.   4. Astonished at what she had heard, she did not know what to say.   5. I can see the dog chewing a bone.   6. Disappointed with his results, he vowed to do better.   7. Not knowing how to do the work, I left it alone.   8. Searching through an old chest, she found some old but valuable stamps.   9. Seeing an old woman crossing a busy road, the policeman rushed to her aid.   10. Having been warned by the principal, he never did the trick again.   11. Exhausted by the journey, he did not mind where he slept.   12. Thinking over a past amusing incident, she laughed out loud.   13. Not being angry with her anymore, he spoke to her again.

Chapter 17　解答

17–2 小練習

1. are　2. are　3. are　4. are; aren't　5. are; Isn't　6. is; is　7. are; is　8. is; are　9. is
10. are　11. am; Are　12. are　13. is　14. is; are　15. is; am　16. is; is　17. is; is　18. are; are; are

17–3 小練習

1. are; are　2. is　3. are　4. are　5. is; are; is　6. is; Isn't　7. are; is　8. are　9. are
10. are　11. is; is　12. is; is　13. is; is　14. is; are　15. is; is　16. is; are　17. are　18. is

應用練習

PART 1

1. are; are　2. are; is; is　3. is; is　4. is; is　5. is; Are　6. are; is　7. is　8. is; is　9. is; is
10. is; are　11. is　12. are; is　13. is; is　14. is; is　15. is; is　16. are　17. is　18. are

PART 2

1. are; Is　2. is　3. is　4. are　5. is　6. is　7. are　8. is; are　9. is　10. are　11. are
12. are; is　13. are　14. are　15. are　16. is; is　17. is; is　18. isn't; is　19. is; are　20. is; is

PART 3

1. are   2. is   3. is   4. is; is   5. is   6. are; are   7. are; are   8. is; is   9. are; is   10. is; is

11. is; is   12. isn't   13. is; are   14. is; are   15. is; are   16. is; is   17. is   18. are   19. is; is

20. are; is

PART 4

1. have   2. has   3. has; is   4. is; are   5. has; has   6. are; has; has   7. have; are   8. is; has

9. is; are   10. are; is; is/are   11. have; have   12. is   13. is/are; are   14. are; is   15. has; is; have; are

16. are; is   17. are; is; has   18. is; have; is; has   19. is; has

PART 5

1. were   2. was; has   3. have; Don't   4. Has; does   5. was; Have   6. does; do; has

7. was; don't   8. has; has   9. Has; does   10. was   11. was   12. were   13. were   14. was

15. was; wasn't   16. were   17. were; was   18. was; was   19. were; were   20. was; were

21. were; wasn't   22. was

PART 6

1. is   2. is   3. is; is   4. is; is; is   5. is; respects   6. is; have   7. is; are; have; is   8. is; is

9. is ; comes; washes; are   10. is; think; are; fails   11. is; occurs; is; are   12. is; keeps   13. is; are

14. is; replaces; comes   15. have   16. has   17. does; is

PART 7

1. flashes; is   2. has; are   3. lasts; are   4. want   5. knows; is   6. are; is   7. has; thinks; are

8. does; seems   9. were; was   10. does ; are   11. keeps; gives   12. approaches; seems   13. goes; is

14. costs; are   15. says; is   16. has; have   17. has; has   18. is   19. grow; need; is; survives

20. are; delivers

PART 8

1. says; is; is; listens   2. have; is; feel; is   3. is; provides; carry   4. is; catch   5. is; is   6. is; are

7. cost; costs   8. have; have   9. is; are; needs   10. likes; are   11. breathes; draws; diffuses; reaches

12. is; is   13. is; collect; is   14. enables   15. is; is   16. varies   17. listens; says; does   18. is; counts

19. comes; want   20. has

PART 9

1. are   2. is   3. are   4. are   5. is   6. is; is   7. are; is   8. is; is   9. is   10. is   11. are

12. is   13. is   14. are   15. are   16. is   17. is; are   18. are

PART 10

1. do   2. has   3. has; have   4. do; has   5. have   6. do   7. have   8. have   9. has

10. has; has   11. has   12. has; have   13. has   14. has   15. has   16. has   17. Do   18. has

19. Do; do   20. has

PART 11

1. is   2. have   3. has   4. are   5. have; are   6. are   7. is; have   8. has   9. is   10. is

11. is   12. are; are   13. is; are   14. is   15. seems   16. want; is   17. are   18. are; is   19. has; is; are

20. is

PART 12

1. are; has   2. are; are   3. are; is   4. have   5. have; is   6. has   7. prevails; has   8. are

9. is   10. is; are; is; is   11. is; goes; is   12. are; has; are   13. has; is   14. is   15. are; is   16. has; are

17. are; is

PART 13

1. gives   2. wants; comes; they; grab   3. is; are; their   4. contains   5. has; are   6. is; is

7. comes; comes; is   8. Is; are; is   9. has; his; is   10. are; is; is   11. have; is; are   12. is; comes; he

13.   was; it; was; his   14. is; pass; tells; listen   15. have; their   16. is; it   17. have; they; have

18. they; they   19. has; it   20. is; gives